MURDER OF LOS CAHUILLAS

When Brogan McNally arrives in the sleepy border village of Los Cahuillas he intends to have his horse re-shod and then be on his way. Instead, he finds himself embroiled with a local landowner, James Brindley, who is intent on taking over the village at all costs — even if it means slaughtering all the inhabitants. Now, with Brindley's manic attentions focused on him, can Brogan save his and the villagers' lives with only his guns to rely on?

L. D. TETLOW

MURDER OF
LOS CAHUILLAS

Complete and Unabridged

LINFORD
Leicester

First published in Great Britain in 2006 by
Robert Hale Limited
London

First Linford Edition
published 2007
by arrangement with
Robert Hale Limited
London

The moral right of the author has been asserted

British Library CIP Data

Tetlow, L. D.
   Murder of Los Cahuillas.—Large print ed.—
Linford western library
   1. Western stories
   2. Large type books
   I. Title
   823.9'14 [F]

ISBN 978–1–84617–777–4

Published by
F. A. Thorpe (Publishing)
Anstey, Leicestershire

Set by Words & Graphics Ltd.
Anstey, Leicestershire
Printed and bound in Great Britain by
T. J. International Ltd., Padstow, Cornwall

This book is printed on acid-free paper

1

'Don't know if they can help or not, old girl,' Brogan McNally said to his horse as he patted her neck. 'In places like this sometimes somebody knows how but most times they don't. I reckon I could do it myself if somebody's got the tools. Don't you worry none though, I'll get you fixed even if I have to walk all the way back to Seattle. I only hope it don't ever come to that though, I left there when I was about fourteen an' ain't never wanted to go back. Don't suppose my old ma is still alive either. Even if she is, I sure as hell wouldn't know her an' she sure as hell wouldn't know me, nor want to, I reckon.'

The reason for Brogan's apparently one-sided conversation with his horse, apart from the fact that he talked to her most of the time, was that she had cast a shoe during the previous day. He was at that moment looking down through the trees on to a small, Mexican-style village, hoping that it had a blacksmith.

He was not in Mexico, but in the territories adjoining the Mexican border there were large sections of the population who were of Mexican or Spanish origin. In fact these territories and Mexico itself were among Brogan's favourite places and he tended to spend a great deal of time there.

He did not lead his horse down into the village straight away; instead he sat on a rock and studied the comings and goings of the village folk. This was quite normal procedure as far as Brogan McNally, saddle tramp, was concerned. Years of drifting had conditioned him to be very wary and time was rarely of any importance.

He had discovered that even seemingly innocent and peaceful communities, such as this appeared to be, sometimes resented men such as he. Although he never meant harm to anyone, he knew that simply being the man he was, leading the life he did, seemed to fill the men in particular with fear or resentment.

He had never quite understood why this should be so. But that was how things were; he accepted it and usually did his best to avoid any form of trouble. It might have been his intention to avoid trouble, but trouble seemed to delight in finding him, which was why he was always cautious.

There was usually at least one trigger-happy man — sometimes a drunk or, more usually, a young buck who was keen to make a name for himself as a gunman and who thought that a saddle tramp would be easy to beat. There was also always the man who thought that the only good saddle tramp was a dead one.

At about fifty years of age Brogan McNally had proved all of them wrong up to that point, but he knew that he was getting no younger and there was always the chance that one day he might just be beaten. Another reason for caution.

It took him about twenty minutes to eventually decide the inevitable, that he had no alternative but to go down into the village. The condition of his horse overrode any other misgivings he might have had. Any further unnecessary walking could easily send her permanently lame. They had been together for a great many years and he did not want to lose her.

By that time he had also worked out that the village had a population approaching 150, including women and children. There was of course, in common with practically every Mexican village he had ever come across, the mandatory church. As yet though, he had seen no sign of a priest.

He was not at all surprised when his approach was relayed to the village almost as soon as he left the cover of the trees and started down the hill. He was seen by a small boy who appeared to be tending goats — a common occupation for small boys. The boy immediately raced down to the village as fast as his little legs and bare feet could take him. By the time Brogan arrived in the village square, there was not a soul to be seen. He was, however, conscious of many pairs of eyes watching his every movement.

This reaction by the villagers was nothing at all unusual; Mexicans in particular always seemed terrified of any stranger, especially gringos, as they called most non-Mexicans. The word had, over the years, changed its real meaning somewhat and had become synonymous with white Americans and non-Spanish Europeans. These days it was more often than not used as a derogatory term. He had also been in many Indian villages and whilst they were also less than welcoming they did not normally run and hide. They simply gazed malevolently at any strangers, something he found far more sinister than running away.

Brogan led his horse to a small trough set against a wall outside the church. A seemingly constant flow of water trickled from a metal tap which had no handle. He did not know if he was supposed to let her drink from the trough or not, sometimes the villagers were resentful of animals drinking from the same source as they did, but at that moment he did not really care. He took off his hat and plunged his head in the cool water.

Immersing his head was normally the closest Brogan McNally ever came to actually washing or bathing. He gulped a mouthful of water, threw back his head, gargled noisily, then spat the water on to the ground. He coughed loudly as he cleared his throat. He glanced around, took another mouthful of water, but this time he drank it.

He eventually straightened up and looked about. Still there was no sign of a priest or anyone else. He was mildly surprised, priests were not normally so reluctant to make their presence known.

'Anybody there?' he called out. Still no reaction. He called out again and when there was yet again no reaction, he drew his gun, went across to the nearest adobe and roughly pushed open the door.

He was quick to adapt to the gloom and saw what seemed to be at least two adults and several children cowering against the far wall. 'You can come out,' he said. 'I don't mean you no harm. I need some help. Leastways my horse needs some help. You do speak English, don't you?'

A small, slim figure came slowly forward and proved to be a girl. Despite her small size he knew that she was probably in her mid-teens. She looked at Brogan's gun with some alarm. Brogan smiled and replaced the gun.

'I speak English, señor,' the girl said.

'Good,' said Brogan. 'Thing is my horse broke a shoe yesterday an' I need somebody to give her a new one. You got a blacksmith in the village?'

'You are not with Señor Brindley?' asked the girl.

'Brindley!' said Brogan. 'No, I ain't

with no Señor Brindley, I ain't with nobody. I ain't never heard of no Señor Brindley either. Do you have somebody who can shoe a horse or not? If you ain't can you tell me the nearest place I can get her seen to?'

'*Sí, señor,*' she replied. 'We have such a man, but I think it is a long time since he has done this. We do not have many horses in the village.'

'As long as he knows what to do, that'll be fine by me an' my old horse,' said Brogan. 'You can tell everybody there ain't no need to be scared of me, I ain't about to shoot nobody or steal nothin' off nobody. All I want is to get my horse fixed an' be on my way.'

The girl said something to the others in Spanish which Brogan did not understand. Although he had found himself in Mexico and the border territories on many occasions, apart from a few odd common words, he had never bothered to learn to speak Spanish.

The family trooped out, led by a

frail-looking, elderly man and a rather large elderly woman. Brogan smiled to himself; elderly Mexican men always seemed to be small and frail whilst most older women were rather large. He had never quite worked out why this should be. The woman smiled weakly at Brogan as she passed. The girl indicated that Brogan should follow her.

He took his horse and was led to the far side of the village where the girl disappeared into an adobe which had a charcoal hearth and various blacksmith's tools outside. After a few moments a man appeared and nodded at Brogan. He said nothing as he bent down, took the horse's hoofs and examined them one by one. He eventually spoke to the girl, who translated.

'He says they are all very old and the others will soon break,' said the girl. 'If you wish he can replace all of them.'

Brogan too examined each hoof, fully expecting to see that the man was trying to fleece him. Instead he found himself agreeing with the blacksmith. Two of the shoes were very thin.

'OK, I guess so,' said Brogan. 'How much?'

The girl spoke to the blacksmith. 'Two dollars,' she said.

'Is that for all four or each?' asked Brogan.

Again she spoke to the blacksmith. 'Two dollars, that is for the four of them,' she said.

'You got yourself a deal,' said Brogan. 'Sure sounds a reasonable price to me. I'll leave the horse here. Is there anywhere I can get me a bite to eat while I'm waitin'?'

'Bite to eat?' she queried.

'Yeah, you know, food,' he said indicating his mouth.

'Ah, *sí, señor*,' she said with a broad smile. 'I did not understand *bite*. There is only the cantina. It is owned by my uncle. I am sure they will be able to find you some food.'

'Then lead me there,' said Brogan. As a precaution he removed his Winchester rifle from the saddle holster. Such weapons were very expensive and eagerly sought after and it was never safe to leave them unattended. Although he had always found Mexican peasants to be very honest, he was not prepared to risk losing it. 'Does this place have a name?' he asked.

'Los Cahuillas,' she replied.

'Los Cahuillas,' repeated Brogan 'And your name?'

'Maria,' she replied again. 'And you are . . . *señor*?'

'McNally, Brogan McNally,' said Brogan. 'You can call me Brogan. Just plain Brogan will do.'

'Oh, no, *señor*,' she replied, obviously very self-conscious. 'You are an old man, it would not be fitting for one as young as me to be so familiar. I must call you Señor Brogan or Señor McNally.'

'An old man!' exclaimed Brogan. He looked at the girl and suddenly laughed. 'Yeah, I guess I am at that compared to you. OK, Señor Brogan it is. Just don't call me Señor McNally. That would make me feel really old.'

'Thank you, Señor Brogan,' she said, apparently rather confused. 'Come, I am sure the cantina will have some good food.'

By the time Maria ushered him into the cantina, life in the village appeared to have returned to something like normality, although many still looked at Brogan with a wary eye. She spoke to another large woman, who seemed to indicate that she did have food. Maria then left, promising that she would be back before he had finished his meal.

There was not a lot of choice; she could apparently provide a meat stew, a rice dish or bread and cheese. Since Brogan quite enjoyed rice he settled for an otherwise unknown spicy rice dish rather than dry bread and cheese or the stew which seemed to be more vegetables than meat. His rice dish also proved to be mainly rice and vegetables with the mearest hint of meat, either goat or sheep, but, although very spicy, it tasted very good.

It certainly made a change from his diet of herbs, roots, bulbs and the occasional rabbit, snake or lizard, which had been his fare for the previous month or more. He also had the choice of coffee or a cloudy-looking local alcoholic drink which she called *beer* although it seemed to Brogan this was all it had in common with normal beer. He settled for the coffee. He fully expected what was known as prairie coffee — a local infusion of herbs and seeds — but was pleasantly surprised when given real coffee.

'That was good,' he said, smiling appreciatively at the large woman who served him. 'How much?' Knowing that he would not be able to understand her, he took a handful of coins from his pocket and held it out for her to take what she wanted. She took two ten-cent coins. 'Very cheap,' he said again. 'Mind, I don't suppose you got that much need for money out here.' His words were plainly lost on the woman.

At that moment Maria returned.

'Your horse will be ready in a few minutes, señor,' she said. 'It is getting late, do you wish to stay here in the cantina for the night? There is a room with beds which travellers sometimes use. We do not get many travellers.'

'I don't think so,' he said. 'I'm more at home out under the trees or in a barn. Me an' beds don't really get on. They usually make my back ache. 'Sides, I prefer the bugs outside.'

'Bugs, *señor*?' she queried.

'Yeah, bugs, ticks, fleas an' things. You know, things what make you itch,' he tried to explain. He went through the motions of scratching himself which plainly confused Maria even more. 'Trouble with beds is you never know who had the bugs before you. Out in the open they seem different somehow.'

'I think you make the fun with me, Señor Brogan,' she said. 'I do not understand what is bugs.'

'It don't matter,' said Brogan with a broad grin. 'I prefer somewhere in the open air, that's all, or maybe a barn if it's rainin'.'

'*Sí*, I understand,' she said. '*Sí*, there are many such places you can sleep. I am sure that nobody will mind.'

'What about your padre or even a sheriff?' asked Brogan. 'Most priests an' almost every sheriff I ever met don't like the idea of strangers in their towns or villages.' He laughed. 'With priests I ain't never been sure if it's the stranger or their women they don't trust.'

'We have no sheriff and sadly, we no longer have a priest,' said Maria with a sigh. 'He was killed by Señor Brindley's men three days ago. He was buried only this morning.'

'Señor Brindley, again,' said Brogan. 'Who the hell is this Brindley? With a name like Brindley I'd say he wasn't Spanish or Mexican. Mind, that don't always mean much. I once knew a Spaniard named Phillips an' two Mexicans named Jones an' Cartwright.'

'No, Señor Brindley is neither Spanish nor Mexican,' said Maria. 'He is

Americano, a gringo. He owns a big ranch not far from here. He has many cattle and horses.'

'And why should he kill your padre?'

'I think it was because Father Alonso told him that he was going to talk to the governor,' said Maria. 'There has been much trouble. I do not know all the details. If you wish to know more you must ask Señor Gramali. He is the village headman. It is not fitting for me to tell you. I am only a young girl and women and girls do not know about these things. That is for the men.'

'I reckon you know a darned sight more'n you'd ever let on,' said Brogan. 'OK, maybe I will ask him, maybe I won't. Whatever it is ain't got nothin' to do with me that's for sure. OK, let's go see if my horse is ready.'

Despite the fact that Brogan was well aware that it was none of his business, he was curious. In fact he had to admit to himself that it amounted to something more than pure curiosity. It invariably did.

He was like that, seemingly unable to keep his nose out of other people's business and almost always taking the part of the apparent underdog. He knew he ought to know better and always vowed never to become involved again. It had happened many times but despite his intentions, he never seemed to learn. His curiosity almost always led to trouble being very close behind.

His horse was indeed ready and was actually eating her way through a meal of bran, corn and oats. Brogan smiled and gave the blacksmith an extra twenty-five cents to cover the cost of the feed.

'He says the horse can remain here for the night,' said Maria. 'There is shelter at the back of the house. He also says that you too can sleep with your horse if you wish. There will be no charge for either of you. For the horse he can supply feed but not for you. You must eat at the cantina if you require food.'

'Sounds fair enough to me,' said

Brogan. 'OK, tell him thanks. Now don't you think you should be gettin' back to your folk. They might be gettin' the wrong idea about me an' you.'

Maria suddenly became very self-conscious and obviously blushed. She hurriedly left him alone.

★   ★   ★

For the remaining two hours or so of daylight, Brogan wandered round the village. A short distance away there was a river, not very wide or deep, across which there was a ford and a narrow footbridge — in actual fact more a series of planks. An elderly man and two boys were fishing a little further upstream.

The land appeared to be reasonably fertile and supported a variety of crops, principal of which seemed to be corn. All in all, Los Cahuillas was a rather more prosperous village than a great many he had come across.

Out of nothing more than idle

curiosity — he was most certainly not a religious man — he looked inside the church. As ever, it was simple and plain but, again as ever, spotlessly clean. There was a small adobe next to the church which he took to be the priest's house.

Seeing the church and the house made him wonder why the priest had been killed. Even the most hard-bitten outlaw, be he Mexican or gringo, rarely killed priests and American cattle-ranchers did not normally bother with them at all. However, Maria had told him that the priest had been shot by Brindley's men and he had no reason to doubt her.

'Now hold on!' he suddenly said to himself. 'That's dangerous thinkin', McNally. It ain't none of your business what happened or why. For all you know Padre Alonso was a complete bastard an' deserved what he got. You've met a few so-called religious men just like that.'

About an hour later he found himself

outside the cantina and it seemed that there were quite a few people inside. He decided to risk sampling the cloudy liquid he had been offered earlier. As he entered, complete silence fell on the room and at least forty pairs of eyes stared at him.

'Don't mind me,' he said to nobody in particular, 'I just fancy me a drink. You all carry on an' ignore me.' A buzz of conversation gradually built up and Brogan knew that he was the only topic.

'We have beer, whiskey, gin or rum,' said a large man speaking good English and standing beside a shelf containing several barrels and bottles. 'I also have tequila but I think you will not like. Most gringos do not like tequila. You are Señor Brogan McNally, no?'

'I am Señor Brogan McNally, yes,' said Brogan. 'I ate here earlier.'

'*Sí*, this I know,' replied the man. 'Maria and my wife, they tell me. Maria is the daughter of my brother. My name is Jose. You wish to see Maria?' His manner was almost challenging. 'There is no need, I speak the very good English.'

'Indeed you do,' agreed Brogan. 'No, I don't need Maria. All I want is a drink. I'll try your beer.' He held out a handful of coin and allowed the man to take what he wanted.

'Maria is a good girl,' said the man as he poured the cloudy liquid into a metal tankard. 'All girls in Los Cahuillas are good girls.' Again Brogan felt that he was being challenged or even warned. 'You leave tomorrow?'

'Probably,' said Brogan. 'I had thought about stayin' a day or two since I've been on the move every day for about a month. I reckon me an' my old horse deserve a good rest.'

'I think it is better if you leave tomorrow,' said the man.

Brogan smiled and shook his head. 'Don't you worry none about me,' he said. 'I ain't lustin' after your women or girls. They don't normally interest me and when they do I stick to older women.'

21

'That is not why I tell you it is better to leave tomorrow,' said Jose. 'Tomorrow Señor Brindley comes to the village. It would be better for your health if you were not here. I do not think he will like a stranger being here. He does not like any strangers.'

'Seems he don't like priests either,' said Brogan. 'I hear he killed your Father Alonso.'

'*Sí*,' said Jose. 'It was not Brindley himself, it was one of his men, but he was told to do it by Brindley. Padre Alonso, he was going to see the governor.'

'About what?' asked Brogan.

Jose looked very uneasy and called across to one of the others. 'This is Miguel Gramali,' he said.

'The village headman,' said Brogan. 'Maria has told me about you.'

'That girl she knows too much,' muttered Gramali. 'I too have heard about you, Señor McNally. I have seen you walking in the village. It is not often we see strangers in Los Cahuillas. I hope you will take the advice. You are leaving tomorrow, no?'

'Everybody suddenly wants to see the back of me,' said Brogan. 'I know I'm only a dirty, smelly saddlebum, but I'm sure that ain't the reason.'

'It is for your own safety, señor,' said Gramali.

'And everybody suddenly seems very concerned about my safety as well,' said Brogan. 'Nobody ain't bothered before, why now? Just in case you hadn't noticed, I'm a big boy now, I can look after myself.'

'Of course you are, señor,' said Gramali. 'But I do not jest when I say it would be better for you. Señor Brindley, he does not appreciate strangers. Already he has killed two of them in one month.'

'Why?' asked Brogan.

Gramali shrugged. 'Who knows?' he said.

'Well somebody sure as hell must know,' said Brogan. 'A man don't normally go round killin' folk just for the hell of it.'

'I do not know why he should do this,' said Gramali. 'Perhaps it was because those men were witness to what he did. I do not know if they were or not. Whatever the reason, they are now buried in our little cemetery. I do not want you to be buried there as well. Besides, we no longer have a priest who can give you a Christian burial. You have heard about Father Alonso? We buried him only this morning.'

'I heard,' said Brogan. 'Two strangers and a priest. All I can say is it must be somethin' pretty damned important. What about your own people, how many of them has he killed?'

'Two only,' said Gramali. 'Both young men who tried to stand up to Señor Brindley. Nobody tries to stand up to him now. We tried with Father Alonso but now he is gone there is nobody.'

'Stand up to what, exactly?' asked Brogan.

'Stand for our rights,' said Gramali. 'We have lived in this land for many,

many years. The problem seems to be that we have no papers saying that the land belongs to us, but we have owned it for over one hundred years — '

'I get it,' interrupted Brogan. 'This Brindley wants you off for some reason. Why should he want you off?'

Gramali shrugged. 'This I do not know, *señor*,' he admitted. 'Father Alonso, he knew but he did not tell us. He promised that he would sort it all out. The only thing he did say was that one day soon we, the people of Los Cahuillas, would all be very rich.'

'Very rich?' queried Brogan. 'I wonder what the hell he meant by that? Is there any gold round here?'

'No gold,' assured the headman. 'No gold, no silver, no nothing.'

'Has anybody checked through Father Alonso's things?' asked Brogan. 'Maybe there somethin' there that'll tell you what's been goin' on.'

'We might be simple farmers, *señor*,' said Gramali, 'but that does not make us fools. We have searched and we found nothing. If there was something there, Señor Brindley he found it first. When his men shot Father Alonso, he searched the house. I do not know what they found or even if they found anything.'

'You can bet your sweet life they did,' said Brogan. 'Either that or he made certain they couldn't find it.'

2

The following morning Brogan was up at his normal time, just as the first rays of light were casting long shadows across the valley. He had spent a comfortable night on a pile of straw alongside his horse and under the small lean-to at the rear of the blacksmith's adobe.

The question of Padre Alonso and what he knew about James Brindley had occupied his thoughts for a short time the previous night, but not for too long. He had an ability to switch off his thoughts and even emotions almost at will and he often did, even in the saddle. When he did it in the saddle it was nearly as good as sleeping except that his senses were fully alert.

The first thing he did was to immerse his head in a tub of water and take a good drink. The second thing was go to

Padre Alonso's adobe alongside the church. There he was quite surprised to discover that he was not the first to arrive. Miguel Gramali, the village headman and Jose from the cantina were already searching.

'Found anythin'?' asked Brogan.

'As yet, no, Señor McNally,' admitted Gramali. 'At least, not anything which might explain why Señor Brindley wants this land. We have searched before and found nothing but when you said that Father Alonso might have hidden anything he had, we decided to search again. What we have discovered so far is a large gold crucifix hidden behind a loose block. It is plainly gold and must be very expensive, but it is not so expensive as to make the whole village very rich.' He handed the crucifix to Brogan.

'Looks like gold right enough,' agreed Brogan weighing it expertly in his hand. 'It feels like gold too. Gold somehow feels different from other metals. It's quite heavy, but as you say, even if it is solid gold, it's not heavy enough to make you all rich. No, I think you must look for papers, possibly some official papers, but I doubt if there'd be anythin' like that. More than likely it'll be some of Father Alonso's own notes.' He handed the crucifix back to Gramali. 'I'd still keep quiet about this if I was you,' he added. 'I'm sure Brindley wouldn't refuse it.'

'You are right, Señor McNally, we have found nothing,' said Jose. 'I think that Señor Brindley must have discovered it, if there was ever anything to discover. You are right about the crucifix too. If he knew about it he would most certainly take it from us. We will keep it safe.'

'Perhaps what Father Alonso knew was kept in his mind,' said Gramali. 'There are no books, only two Holy Bibles and a register. We did not know about the register. It lists all the births, deaths and marriages in Los Cahuillas since before Father Alonso first came. It is unusual because I know of no other villages which had such a register even before you gringos came. Even now most do not. Some of the towns and cities have one but even there they are not very common and it is usually only the rich and important people who have such details recorded. The poor and peons such as us are not worth keeping records about in either Mexico or America. We have searched through all the pages of both the Bibles and the register. There is nothing hidden.'

'You must leave, Señor McNally,' said Jose 'We know that Señor Brindley comes today. I think he comes to tell us that we must leave this village. It is said that he has bought this land.'

'And he does not come alone,' added Gramali. 'He never comes alone. He will not like it when he sees you, he does not like any strangers. He has been known to kill them even when they had nothing to do with him.'

'What about the law, a marshal or a sheriff, even the army?' asked Brogan. 'There must be somebody. This is

America, not Mexico.'

'There is nobody,' said Gramali. 'Señor Brindley, *he* is the only law. We might all be *Americanos* now, but the American government does not yet seem to know this. You must leave, Señor McNally. He will be here soon.'

'An' I don't allow no man to scare me off,' said Brogan, defiantly. 'I'll leave when I'm good and ready. I ain't never run yeller yet an' I sure as hell am too old to change my ways now.'

'If you do not leave, perhaps it will be that you will never leave here,' said Jose. 'You will become a permanent resident in our cemetery.'

'That's a chance I'll have to take,' said Brogan. 'How come he was able to buy this land with you here?'

Miguel Gramali laughed. 'We do not know for certain if this is so,' he said. 'it is only rumour. We do not matter, Señor McNally, the poor do not count for anything and peons such as we count for even less than a grain of sand. We might have lived on these lands for

31

many years, long before the gringos arrived, and it is claimed that we have the blood of the old Indians in our veins, but that means nothing. We have no papers to prove that we own the land. We now have a register but I think it will mean nothing. Unfortunately it does not prove ownership of anything but our names. Has not the same thing happened with the Indian tribes in the north and even here in the south? They have had their land taken from them. The gringos they now control our lives. Father Alonso, he went to the court but could not prove anything. The court says that the government can do what it will with our land. Unfortunately there are even some of our own people who also consider us to be worthless. They too take much land.'

'I just wish I knew what was so darned important about this place,' said Brogan. 'There sure don't seem to be anythin' special about it. Keep lookin', you just might find somethin'.'

Brogan wandered over to the cantina

where he had a mug of coffee and something called a tortilla. It was very bland but it filled his stomach. While he was eating, Maria arrived.

'My uncle, he is very concerned that you will not leave Los Cahuillas, Señor Brogan,' she said. 'I too am worried. Señor Brindley, he will come soon. It is quite possible that he will kill you.'

'And that bothers you?' asked Brogan. 'I'm flattered, Maria. I suppose if I had a lick of sense I'd get the hell out of it. Only thing is, I'm a stubborn old man an' the older I get the more stubborn I become. I ain't never run scared from no man yet an' I don't intend to start now.'

'My father too, he was very stubborn,' said Maria. 'He too was very proud, just like you, Señor Brogan. He always knew better than anybody, nobody was able to tell him what to do. One day he was given a horse in the will of an old uncle. He had never owned a horse before but he was quite certain that he could ride it. He always said it was no different from riding a mule. The only problem was that the horse did not want my father to ride it, it did not want any man to ride it. My father he was thrown from the horse many times but still he insisted that he would ride it and still the horse threw him off. One day, when he was thrown, he hit his head on a rock. We buried my father the next morning.'

'What happened to the horse?' asked Brogan.

'Oh, many people have said that he tasted very nice,' said Maria with a broad grin.

'Sorry about your father,' said Brogan.

'Do not be sorry, señor,' she said. 'I was only four years old. I do not remember anything. My two older brothers, my young sister and myself have been brought up ever since by my grandparents. My mother, she died of the fever just after my father was killed. I tell you this story, señor, because it shows it is sometimes very foolish to do something you have no need to do. My father he did not have to ride that horse, but as far as he was concerned a horse was there to be ridden.'

'Yeah, you're right,' said Brogan with a deep sigh. 'I'd like to know why it's so important for this Brindley to have this land though.'

'It is of no concern to you, Señor Brogan,' said Maria. 'Whatever happens and whatever the reason or the outcome, our problems will still be with us long after you have gone. Your death would be unnecessary. It would be far better if you did not try to ride this particular horse.'

'I guess it would at that,' agreed Brogan, giving her a broad, knowing smile. 'How old did you say you was?'

'I am fifteen years old,' said Maria.

'Fifteen goin' on fifty,' said Brogan. He realized that, young as she was, she was talking nothing but common sense. He was going to change very little by remaining. 'OK, just for you,' he continued, 'I'll forget all about it an' be on my way. I'll go get my horse, at least

I know I can ride her. I won't bother to say farewell to the others. I'll just go. I was thinkin' of restin' up a couple of days but I can see that'd only lead to trouble.'

'It is better that you go,' said Maria. 'I wish you good luck, *señor*.'

Brogan made his way back to the blacksmith's adobe, saddled his horse and slowly headed for the river.

★　★　★

On this occasion, although he could not possibly know otherwise and he had, for once in his life, taken a sensible decision, fate was already against him. Even though he had decided to ride away from Los Cahuillas and its problems, the long tentacles of trouble had already been set in motion.

He had not even reached the ford across the river when a group of five horsemen galloped through. There was no chance of Brogan's being able to avoid them or hide from them. They immediately surrounded him and he wisely offered no resistance.

'Well now, looks like we found us a saddlebum,' leered one of the men, revealing a set of broken and blackened teeth. 'What you doin' in these parts, scum. Bit far out of your usual territory I'd say.'

'Don't have no *usual* territory,' said Brogan. 'Just passin' through. Ain't no law what says a man can't just be passin' through, is there?'

'I suppose you've been in the village all night,' said the leader of the group. 'In that case you've probably heard about me. James Brindley is the name. I own most of this territory.'

'Yeah, I heard 'bout you,' said Brogan. 'Seems you ain't too popular round these parts. Mind, since it seems you own most of it that don't much matter to you, I reckon.'

'Now there speaks a practical man,' said Brindley. 'You're quite right, it doesn't matter a damn what they think. What's your name? If you say Smith or

Jones I won't believe you.'

'Why not?' asked Brogan. 'I guess somebody has to be called Smith or Jones for real. I certainly met me quite few in my time an' they ain't no different from everybody else. But no, it ain't Smith, Jones, Brown or Green, it's McNally, Brogan McNally. Not that that'll mean much to you.'

'You're right about that,' sneered Brindley. 'It doesn't mean a damned thing. Where are you headed?'

'Wherever the fancy takes me,' said Brogan, which was true. It was very rarely that he had a specific destination in mind.

The man who had first confronted Brogan had been eyeing his rifle. Suddenly he moved forward to take it from the saddle holster. Brogan reacted entirely by instinct and before either he or the man fully realized what was happening, the man was staring into the barrel of Brogan's Navy Colt. It all happened so fast that nobody else had moved.

'Now you weren't thinkin' of stealin' my rifle was you?' hissed Brogan. 'If you was, that ain't at all friendly. A man just don't try stealin' another man's rifle, not if he wants to carry on livin'. I knows you wasn't really lookin' to steal it, you just wanted to take a look at it. Well, it's only good manners to ask if you can look. You should always ask first. I've killed men for not askin' first when they probably just weren't thinkin' straight. They might still be alive if they'd only thought an' asked first.'

'Well, it sure ain't goin' to be much use to you when you're dead,' croaked the man.

'That's very true, but then maybe you'd better wait until I am dead,' Brogan hissed again. 'There you go again, doin' things before a man's ready. That's a nasty habit you got there. If I was you I'd be more careful with what you do an' what you say. You might just end up dead before I do, else.'

The man was plainly taken aback by Brogan's stance, and looked very uneasy.

'You asked for it, Jake,' said Brindley with a loud laugh. 'It looks like you've met somebody who isn't scared of you. I'd back off if I were you, I have the feeling that you'd probably come off second best. Saddlebum or no, this feller looks like he knows how to handle himself and a gun. You'll get your chance soon enough. He won't get far but right now there are more important things to attend to.'

'Yeah, I'll get my chance, nothin' more certain,' snarled Jake. 'I know every inch of this territory an' findin' you will be just too easy. That old horse of yours ain't goin' to move very fast. Your days are numbered, McNally. I'll get your rifle an' that Colt. I ain't never owned me a long-barrelled Navy Colt.'

'First you have to kill me,' said Brogan. 'Right now though it's me who has the advantage. I think you must agree with that. Maybe it'll save me a lot of time if I kill you right now.'

Jake licked his lips and slowly moved his horse back a few yards. Brogan smiled and eased back the hammer on his gun. Then he slowly replaced it in his holster.

'You definitely seem to be able to handle yourself and a gun and you plainly don't scare easy,' said Brindley. 'I'm always looking for men who can handle a gun and take orders. Can you take orders, Mr McNally?'

'I don't take orders off no man,' said Brogan. 'Your man was right when he called me a saddlebum. It ain't a term I like but that's what folk call me an' I can't do nothin' about that.' Jake slowly backed further away but Brogan still kept his hand on the handle of his Colt. This did not go unnoticed by Jake or the others and none of them made any attempt to go for their guns. 'Now if you don't mind, Mr Brindley,' continued Brogan, 'I'll be gettin' on my way.'

'Be my guest, Mr McNally,' said Brindley. 'If I were you I'd ride fast and just make sure you keep on riding, for your own sake. Jake has a long memory and he holds a grudge for a long time. There's a chance there'll be some shooting going on in the village, there shouldn't be but you never know with these Mexicans. They're very unpredictable. It isn't any concern of yours why I'm here so don't even look back. Do I make myself clear?'

'As crystal, as they say,' said Brogan. He urged his horse forward and through the ford. 'Good huntin',' he called back. 'You should be OK, I don't think they have anythin' better'n a scatter-gun in the whole village. I dare say even *your* men can handle a scatter-gun an' a few old men, women an' children.'

'Yeah, we can handle 'em,' said one of the other men. 'An' they sure 'nough got themselves a few pretty women an' girls. Maybe you sampled one of 'em already? Now it's our turn.'

Brogan ignored the remark and continued on.

42

He turned by a group of trees and saw the men heading for the church. He immediately dismounted.

'Get all your people out here, Gramali,' ordered Brindley. 'And I mean everybody, includin' children.'

'The children have done nothing,' said Gramali as he came out of an adobe. 'But then neither has anyone else, Señor Brindley.'

'I want them all to hear what I have to say, Gramali,' barked Brindley. 'Get everybody out here. When they are all out, my men will search and anybody found inside will be shot where they are found. That includes any children or women, and anybody who even looks like they might have a gun or even a knife will also be shot. Now get them all out here, Gramali.'

Miguel Gramali called out and slowly the villagers emerged from their adobes. Eventually all the villagers were gathered outside the church.

'We are all here,' Gramali said eventually as he looked around. 'All except one very old man who is near death. He has the fever.'

'Then we might be doing him a favour if we shoot him,' said Brindley. 'Leave the old man alone when you find him,' he instructed his men. 'Don't touch him whatever you do. There's no knowing what the fever is.'

'He is in the third house along the street,' said Gramali.

'Good,' said Brindley. 'Now, you can translate for me, Gramali. I know not everyone speaks English. Now listen to me very carefully, all of you.' He waited for Gramali to translate. 'You have until tomorrow morning to get your things together. I am taking over this village. You can go wherever you like as far as I am concerned but you can't stay here. You can take any sheep, goats or any other animals with you. I sure don't want them.' He allowed Gramali to translate. 'My men are now going to search all the houses.'

'They are going to steal what they can find?' asked Gramali.

'They are going to search,' insisted Brindley. 'They are looking for guns. I can't control what they do with anything else they find. You can't have that much worth stealing, anyhow.'

At a nod from Brindley, his men dismounted and barged their way into the adobes. The process of searching took the best part of an hour and, simply judging by the sounds, consisted of smashing anything which could not be carried. What they were actually looking for they did not seem to know but when they had finished there were two separate piles in the square.

The one consisted of a motley collection of twelve ancient rifles, all old muzzle-loaders, two rather elderly shotguns complete with some cartridges, two ancient flintlock pistols, a collection of knives and even a sword. The other pile consisted of personal and household items which were all too large to find their way into the men's pockets. It was noticeable that there was no cash.

One of the men came out of the cantina waving a bottle. One of the others immediately rushed inside and he too came out with another bottle. The other two men quickly followed and soon all four were parading about the square drinking from their prizes and leering at any woman who was unfortunate enough to catch their eye. In all this James Brindley remained astride his horse.

'I will be back in the morning, Gramali,' said Brindley. 'You'd best all be ready to leave or even be on your way. Anything or anyone left inside your houses will be burned along with the house and that includes old men dying of fever.'

'What about your men, *señor?*' asked Gramali. 'Are they to stay here?'

'Well I haven't anything else for them to do right now,' said Brindley. 'Where or how they decide to spend their free time is up to them.' He called to the men. 'Just don't go burnin' their hovels down before the morning. I promised they wouldn't be and I am a man of my word.'

'Yes, sir, Mr Brindley, sir,' replied Jake. 'We'll just make sure they makes 'emselves ready to leave. There's enough whiskey an' rum an' food in the cantina to keep us goin'. No need to worry 'bout us.'

'No, I don't suppose there is,' said Brindley with a laugh.

Brogan moved his horse behind a clump of bushes and waited for James Brindley to pass and get well out of sight. So far he had seen nothing that any interference on his part might have changed. However, with their boss out of the way, he had the feeling that this state of affairs might not continue. He left his horse amongst the bushes and made his way towards the village.

'You heard what Mr Brindley said,' barked Jake. 'Start gettin' your things together an' be ready to leave in the mornin'.'

Gramali spoke to the villagers in Spanish and all slowly returned to their adobes. Small boys were sent out to the outlying countryside to bring in what few goats and sheep they owned. Two rickety wagons and about ten mules appeared, the only form of transport the villagers had.

By this time Brogan had managed to get himself inside the church and had clambered up into the small bell-tower. From here he had an almost completely uninterrupted view of the whole village. Brindley's men were lounging under the only tree in the village square, no more than ten yards from the church.

His instinct was to somehow help the people, but he had seen enough of very similar situations to know that any short-term intervention would be a waste of time. However, and for reasons known only to himself, he remained where he was.

What few religious artefacts there were in the church were collected by a couple of elderly women, although they did not look up, for which Brogan was rather grateful. It might have proved difficult for the women not to reveal where he was, even to their menfolk.

Brogan guessed that he had been up in the cramped hole that was the bell-tower for about four hours. Up to that point, none of the four men had attempted to interfere with the villagers in any way and, although they each had a bottle of drink, they did not appear to be any the worse for it. He did, however, wonder exactly how long that state of affairs might last. None of the four made any attempt to hide their feelings or comments from the younger women as they passed. In fact at least two of the women seemed to be actively inviting comment.

Late in the afternoon one of the men demanded that they be brought some food and Brogan was not too surprised when the two women who appeared to be inviting attention brought it to them. Brogan also noted that neither woman complained when it was obvious that they allowed the men's hands to wander under their skirts.

'That's what I call askin' for trouble,' Brogan said to himself. 'Even if Brindley's men don't give you no more trouble it's a sure bet your menfolk will when you're away from here. They can see what you're doin'.'

Suddenly Jake and one of the men decided that the chance of two apparently very willing young women was too much to resist. They each grabbed hold of a woman each and dragged them — each woman feigning resistance — into the church. Brogan had the perfect view.

Normally he would have tried to help but in this case he felt that it was exactly what the women wanted and in any case no better than they deserved. However, his attention was drawn back to the square where the other two men had also decided to emulate their companions. This time, however, the women were plainly not at all willing.

The first two women they attempted to grab actually managed to escape, something which seemed to amuse the men. This escape was a signal to all the other women of the village to hide, but it did not deter the men.

They burst into the nearest adobe and dragged out two screaming figures. It was at that moment that Brogan knew he had to act. The first girl to be dragged out and towards the church, was Maria.

3

Strangely, although she had at first screamed, Maria appeared to put up less resistance than the other girl, although she was plainly far from willing. If nothing else she seemed resigned to what was about to happen to her. What little resistance had been shown by the first two women was obviously put on for nothing more than effect. Their resistance had completely evaporated once they were inside the church and out of sight of the village. Brogan caught a glimpse of Maria's face and saw a look of complete hatred. A rare sight in one so young.

The second girl was about the same age as Maria but she was crying and plainly terrified. Even so, she struggled, screamed and knew enough of where to hurt a man as she attempted to kick the man in the groin. All this did was to seemingly make the man more determined and excited.

However, her struggles and screams were in vain. As soon as the two girls were dragged from their adobes, the entire village suddenly emptied of the few who were about. Apart from the screams, the village had become deathly silent. Even the dogs had disappeared. Brogan knew that most of them were probably just thankful that it was not them or theirs who were about to be assaulted.

By that time the two men on the floor of the church were well and truly occupied and appeared hardly to notice as the other men dragged the two girls inside. Brogan had drawn his pistol but was finding it difficult, especially in the confined space, to get a good line on the man about to take Maria.

Actually he could probably have shot one of the two men already in the church far more easily than either of the two who had just entered. Unusually for Brogan though, his mind was concentrated on Maria almost to the exclusion of all else. This was rare, but it did happen on occasion.

He had just managed to get a good line on the man grappling with Maria when she seemed to choose that precise moment to put up some real resistance. There was now too much movement and there was a distinct danger of Brogan shooting her. He could do little but wait for a better opportunity.

That opportunity came when the man suddenly succeeded in getting Maria on to the floor and forcing up her skirts. He then forced himself over her and gave a coarse, triumphant laugh.

Shooting a man in the back was not normally the way Brogan chose to kill any man. For some strange reason he had always had a sense of what was fair and right and back-stabbing or shooting was not, in his opinion, quite right. He always felt that shooting in the back was something of a coward's way and most definitely a method of last resort.

However, on this occasion, being

where he was, wedged in a small space alongside the bell and with very little room to move his arms, he felt that he had no alternative.

The single shot echoed round the empty church, the man slumped lifeless on top of Maria and for a very brief moment the other men looked round in panic and horror. The two women suddenly screamed and tried desperately to push the men off them and, even though they could not see Brogan, tried to cover their modesty. Maria and the other girl simply sank to the floor.

Suddenly the three remaining men roughly pushed aside their victims and searched for their guns. Jake looked up, leapt to his feet, trying to drag up his pants whilst firing his gun at Brogan. The bullet ricocheted off the bell, causing Brogan to wince at the noise. Jake had by that time disappeared but Brogan managed to get in one more shot as a man passed fleetingly below him. His line, although taken very quickly, was very accurate and another man died.

There were two more shots, apparently from outside the church, both of which hit the bell, creating a deafening ringing, This forced Brogan to crouch as tight as he could with his hands clamped to his ears. In a purely natural reaction, he also closed his eyes.

When the ringing had stopped he glanced from the bell-tower down on to the village square. Jake and the one remaining man were racing for their horses. Brogan did not try to shoot, by that time they were at the extreme range of his Colt and there was neither the time nor the space to use his Winchester. The two men leapt on their horses and raced out of the village.

'Ah, well,' he said to himself. 'Looks like you're stuck with it now, don't it, McNally? You'll never learn, will you? You should've just kept your nose out of their business an' just kept on goin'. Brindley ain't goin' to let this go so easy, that's for sure.'

'Is that you, Señor Brogan?' a voice called through the jangle of noise still reverberating in his head. 'I think it must be you, *señor*, I know of no other man who would do such a thing.'

'Sure is,' replied Brogan. 'Looks like a good job I came back. Are you OK? How about the other girl?'

'I am well,' said Maria. 'Elsa, she also is well but I think she is very frightened. She has never seen a man shot before.'

'And you have?' asked Brogan, suspecting that he knew the answer as he clambered down from the tower.

'*Sí*, I have,' said Maria in a matter-of-fact way.

'Seems to me you've seen or done most things,' said Brogan, not bothering to ask any details. He dusted himself down and looked at the two older women who appeared very uncertain as to what he was going to do next. 'I reckon you two just about got what you came for,' he said to them.

Maria glanced at both women scornfully. 'They do not speak English,' she said, 'but I think they know what you mean. They know you saw what really happened. It is true, they are both well-known for being only too willing to go with men — any man. Carla, she has a small child but no husband. It is not known who the father of her child is and I think she also does not know for certain. They always blame the man of course.'

'Then I reckon most folk'll know what happened to them in here an' why,' said Brogan. 'In the meantime you'd better get Elsa back to her parents and tell them that nothing happened to her.'

'*Sí*, I will do this,' said Maria. 'For myself and Elsa, she is my cousin, I must thank you. I thought you had left us.'

'Just as well I had second thoughts then, ain't it,' said Brogan. 'The only thing is I've probably stirred up a whole lot more trouble than you might've had, trouble for the village I mean. Brindley is sure to blame you all for what happened. Still, at least I saved you from being raped.'

'Women have suffered such things since the beginning of time and lived,' said Maria. 'But I am proud of my chastity and did not want to lose it in such a violent way. I thank you.'

'How old did you say you was — fifteen?' mused Brogan. He suddenly stopped and listened. 'It sounds like we got company,' he said.

In confirmation of this, two timid faces appeared at the church door, each man carrying his sombrero. They carried them simply because it was the custom for men to remove their hats when entering a church.

'I told Jose that it could only be you, Señor McNally,' said Miguel Gramali. 'We thought you had left us.'

'Good job I came back,' said Brogan. 'At least I saved two of your girls from being raped. I can't say much about the other two, don't think they know the meanin' of the word.'

Gramali and Jose glanced at the two women but said nothing to them. The women smiled thinly at Brogan, adjusted their blouses and ran out into the square. Brogan heard various comments, mainly from other older women, and could probably have taken a well-informed guess as to what was being said going purely by the tone of their voices. Maria and Elsa also left but were not subjected to any form of verbal abuse.

'We thank you for what you have done, Señor McNally,' said Gramali. 'Now I think we must all leave Los Cahuillas very quickly. Perhaps if we are not here when Señor Brindley returns he will not bother with us.'

'I wouldn't count on it,' said Brogan. 'I know it'll really be me he wants but men like that have a habit of takin' their feelin's out on them least able to defend 'emselves.' He turned over the two bodies with his foot and nodded. 'Still, he's now got two less men to bother you with.'

'These two will make little difference,' said Gramali. 'I do not know for certain how many men he has, but I know he can find more. You have seen what weapons we have, Señor McNally, we cannot defend ourselves against even two good rifles. Leaving now is the only chance we have.'

'Just like that,' said Brogan, with a deep sigh. 'Maybe it would've been easier just to have let 'em do what they wanted with Maria and Elsa.'

Jose shrugged. 'Unfortunately, it might well have been easier,' he said. 'I am sure Elsa, Maria and their families are most grateful to you, *señor*, but they are only a small part of the community. Now two of Señor Brindley's men are dead. I think all our people must suffer for this.'

Brogan looked down at the two bodies and picked up their pistols. 'You've got two good guns now,' he said. 'There's even about twenty bullets for each gun. There might even be more in their saddle-bags.'

'Two guns, even good ones, in the hands of men who do not how to fight or kill are of little use, *señor*,' muttered

Gramali. 'We are but simple farmers. Most find killing even a bird or a fox very difficult. Our religion tells us that all life is sacred and it is not for man to take another life.'

'I give up,' said Brogan with a resigned sigh. 'You slaughter sheep an' goats don't you?'

'That is for food only,' said Gramali. 'We do not eat men.'

'So you're prepared to let them slaughter you?' said Brogan. 'OK, I've done my best, there's nothin' else I can do. I'm leavin' an' this time I ain't comin' back no matter what happens to any of you.'

'Please, Señor McNally, do not be too hasty,' said Jose. 'Of course, Miguel is right in many ways but Padre Alonso was quite certain that if necessary we must defend ourselves. I have heard him say that sometimes it is impossible not to kill and that it is permissible to kill to defend your family. No, Señor McNally, and I think I speak for most people in the village, I now know we must make a stand against Señor Brindley.'

'That would be madness,' objected Gramali. 'We shall all be slaughtered. This time two of our young women were saved from a terrible fate. Next time they will not be so lucky. All the women of the village are in danger.'

'But we shall be slaughtered even if we leave now,' said Jose. 'He will not rest until we are dead. We might as well stay here and die fighting while we defend our homes and families.'

'You talk pure madness,' insisted Gramali.

'Well there sure ain't nothin' I can do about it if you don't want any help,' said Brogan. 'I suggest you get yourselves sorted out. I'm goin' to find my horse. When I come back I expect you to have decided what you want to do. All I will say is that if you want me to stay an' help, I will. I mean, it ain't goin' to make much difference where they kill me.'

'You talk of dying in a very casual

manner, Señor McNally,' said Gramali. 'Does it not bother you?'

'We all got to die sometime,' replied Brogan. 'Like everybody else though, I don't intend goin' before I have to. Now you decide what the hell you're goin' to do next an' I'll see if I can help.'

Brogan left them looking at each other and stomped off towards the river. On the way he was joined by two small, grinning boys.

'You kill Señor Brindley?' asked one of them. 'My papa he say you must kill Señor Brindley.'

'Your papa he talk too much,' muttered Brogan. 'Maybe your papa he should kill Señor Brindley. Hell, I'm even talkin' like you now. Tell me somethin', son,' he said, smiling at the boy. 'Why is it that you still call everybody *señor* even when you hate their guts?'

'*Hate their guts?*' the boy asked, plainly mystified by the question. 'I do not understand what you mean, *señor*.'

'Why do you call everybody *señor*, even people you don't like.'

'I still do not understand,' insisted the boy. 'All men are *señor* and all women are *señora* or *señorita*. Perhaps you *Americanos* have another word. What else would you have us call them?'

'Nothin' else, I guess,' said Brogan. 'Tell you what, son, you can both go fetch my horse for me. She's over in that far clump of bushes, at least that's where I left her. I'm thirsty an' that water looks nice an' cool.'

'*Sí, señor*,' said the boy. 'We fetch your horse.'

They ran off, splashing noisily through the ford instead of using the bridge, leaving Brogan to scoop a mouthful of water and reflect on what had happened and what he was going to do next.

About five minutes later the boys reappeared leading Brogan's old horse and once again they splashed through the ford.

'Señor,' said the boy who could speak English, 'We think there is somebody watching the village. I think it is one of the two men who ran away from you. I saw his face.'

'I can't say as I'm surprised,' admitted Brogan. The fact that he had sent the boys to fetch his horse held no particular significance. There had been no thought in his mind about anyone hiding. 'I suppose he saw you?' he asked.

'Oh, *sí*,' replied the boy. 'Pablo, he saw him first. I do not think he was expecting us.' He proudly puffed out his small chest. 'He must have been very frightened of me and Pablo because he ran away.'

'Ran?' queried Brogan.

'*Sí, señor*,' said the boy. 'We did not see his horse.'

Brogan laughed. 'Sure, you must've scared the hell out of him. Well done.' He mounted his horse. 'Maybe I'd better go take a look myself. It might be safer if you two went back to the village.'

'We can help you look for him, señor,' said the boy. 'We both know this area very well. There are many places for a man to hide. We know where to look, you do not.'

'I don't think so, son,' said Brogan. 'If you scared him that much, next time he sees you he might just be so scared he'll try an' shoot you.'

'But, señor . . . .' insisted the boy.

'No, son,' snapped Brogan. 'I don't want your pa blamin' me if you get yourselves shot. Now do as you're told an' get back to the village.'

'Sí, señor,' mumbled the boy.

Brogan laughed and urged his horse back through the ford. They've got more guts than most of the older men, he said to himself.

Finding signs of someone having been in hiding amongst the bushes was quite easy to Brogan's experienced eye. Once again he left his horse and moved slowly on foot. The tracks led up to a group of rocks and his instinct told him that the man was still there. There was still no sign of a horse.

Despite the fact that he was now quite certain as to where the man was, Brogan had no intention of pursuing him. As ever, he was cautious and did not see the point of exposing himself to unnecessary danger. He returned to his horse. Suddenly a sound caught his attention and his Colt was in his hand.

He heard the shot and thought he even felt the air move as the bullet passed his head. At that moment the only practical cover he had was his horse.

Normally he would never use his horse as cover but on this occasion he had little alternative. He waited for a second shot but none came. He slowly edged his horse forward, again using her as a shield, until he came to a large tree. He immediately slapped the horse into action and dived behind the tree. At the same time the second expected shot ricocheted off the tree and close to his head. Splinters of bark hit his face.

'That was too close for comfort,' he

muttered to himself. 'Hell, I was sure he was up in them rocks. Just goes to show you is gettin' old, McNally. Now, where the hell are you, Mister?'

He listened and looked intently, but decided that either the man was not moving at all, hardly even breathing, or he had left. He cautiously peered round the bole of his protective tree only to have another bullet thud into the tree close to his head.

'I guess that answers that question,' he muttered. 'I'll say this for you, Mister, you is better than most. Either that or I really must be gettin' old.'

He had no doubt that the shooting had been heard in the village but he knew that he could expect no help from that quarter. He did not blame them; he doubted if there was one of them who was capable of dealing with a man and a good gun.

There was the sound of someone moving to his left but, look as hard as he might, he could not see anyone. He could not even see the tell-tale twitch of a leaf or a branch which was most unusual.

Another bullet thudded into the tree and it came from the same direction as the other two. Brogan was puzzled; the bullets came from one direction, that much was certain, but the sound of somebody moving had come from another direction. He was also quite certain that there had been only one man, which simply served to compound his problem. In addition, his assailant could apparently see him but he could not see his assailant. Such a situation was not uncommon, but it was certainly not the way things normally happened.

Quite obviously, with the man having the advantage, the next move was up to Brogan. He had been in tighter situations, so for the moment he was not too worried, but he plainly could not simply stay where he was. He started to look about, hoping for some inspiration.

There it was again; there was definitely somebody or something moving to his left. However, he had already dismissed its being an animal, since the shooting would have scared an animal off, possibly excluding bears, which were rather nosy as a rule and sometimes, in his experience, even investigated gunfire. He also ruled out a nosy bear simply because this was not bear country. He had been in the general area before and had never seen any signs of bear. Had it been a wolf it would have made off at the first shot.

The sound was repeated, although on this occasion it was definitely a little further away. He decided to call out. It was just possible that whoever it was would answer.

'Who's out there?' he called. 'Who's that movin' about?'

'I ain't movin', McNally,' called a gruff voice from the direction the bullets had come. 'I got you pinned down so it looks like you ain't movin' either.'

'I don't mean you,' Brogan called again. 'There's somebody else movin' about out there.'

The man laughed. 'Nice try, McNally,' he called. 'You don't fool me none though, there's just the two of us. Sure, by now the whole damned village knows there's you an' me out here. Them two stupid kids saw me. Don't matter none though, there ain't nobody goin' to come out here to help you. They is all too shit-scared to do anythin'.'

'OK,' said Brogan, still not con-vinced. 'I was probably just hearin' things. Your friend Jake'll be back soon, I guess.'

'Soon enough,' said the man. 'He'll bring back a few more men an' then it'll be nothin more'n closin' in on you. I'd like to kill you myself, I know exactly where you are. Only reason you ain't dead right now is 'cos you got lucky an' found just about the only tree to hide behind. I ain't no fool though. I knows Brindley was right when he said you knew how to handle a gun, so I ain't about to take no chances. It don't really matter to me who kills you.'

Although the man had him pinned down, Brogan knew that he could not wait until the other men arrived. His mind started to work rapidly. At the same time he tried to locate the exact position of the man and had eventually narrowed him down to being behind one of two large rocks.

The thought crossed his mind that the one way to escape without being seen would be to crawl. He weighed up the angle and line between himself and the rocks and decided that it was just about his only means of escape. He flattened himself and very slowly eased himself forward.

A bullet hit the ground close to his head, sending stinging dust into his eyes. In a flash he was back safely behind the tree.

'Nice idea, McNally,' called the man with a wry laugh. 'Now you know I can see every inch of ground for quite a way round you. Oh, an' don't think about crawlin' away in line with the tree, all I got to do is move my head an' I can see behind that too.'

Brogan remained silent and gave the matter some more thought. He had just decided to get the man to shoot at him again and then play dead. It was a ruse he had used successfully several times in the past. He was just about to show his head when he heard the sounds of somebody moving again.

It was a very slight sound but Brogan's hearing was very keen. On this occasion it came from somewhere very close to where the man was hiding. It sounded as though somebody had slipped on a rock. He waited, wondering if the man had also heard it. Somehow he expected something to happen. He had no idea what that something might be, it was little more than a feeling he had.

Suddenly and most unexpectedly, there were loud, shrill screams quickly followed by a yell of what appeared to be pain and rage from the man. It was all Brogan needed, something or somebody had plainly distracted the man's attention. He raced from behind the tree and up the slight slope towards the rocks. He sensed a bullet as it passed him but suddenly he was crashing over a rock and into the man.

A struggle followed during which both men lost their guns and for a time it was uncertain which of them would prevail. In a brief break the man backed away and, with an almost triumphant snarl, grabbed at a gun close to his feet.

However, his victory was short-lived, as quite suddenly what seemed to be two small bundles hurled themselves on to the man's back. With a loud howl he fell to the ground.

Brogan grabbed at the gun in the man's hand and, panting for breath, stood back, waiting for the small bundles to detach themselves from the man's body. Until they did, he could not shoot for fear of hitting one of them. Eventually the man was on his own and staring fearfully up at Brogan.

'Now just what in hell's name are you two doin' here?' Brogan demanded of the now dusty bundles. 'I thought I told you to go back home.'

'*Sí, señor*,' said the boy who could speak English. 'You told us, but my papa he say I am a very disobedient boy. Sometimes he whips me because I do not do what I am told.'

'Well, you could've got yourself killed,' snarled Brogan.

'*Sí*,' replied the boy with a cheeky grin, 'but we did not and now you are safe. I think this man he kill you if he can.'

'Yeah, you're probably right at that,' said Brogan with a resigned sigh. 'I suppose I have to thank you. It comes to somethin' when I owe my life to a couple of nine- or ten-year-old kids.'

'I am ten years old, *señor*,' said the boy, 'Pablo he is eleven years old.'

'Whatever,' said Brogan. He looked at the man and smiled. 'Looks like you was beaten by a couple of kids as well. I wouldn't tell anybody if I was you, you'd never live down the shame of it.'

4

'OK, so what do I do with you?' Brogan asked his prisoner, obviously not expecting a sensible answer. 'If I had an ounce of sense I'd shoot you right here. It'd probably save a whole heap of trouble later on. Thing is I ain't got that much sense, I just don't shoot unarmed men. That's nothin' more'n murder an' whether you believe me or not, I ain't never done no murder in my life. I killed me plenty of men but they all asked for it or it was self-defence.'

'More fool you,' muttered the man. 'I sure as hell would kill you. Just try me if you don't believe me.'

'Oh, I'm quite certain you would,' said Brogan. 'Thing is, I just can't help bein' a big old softy at heart. You just got lucky, I guess. Since I don't want you an' these good folk don't want you, I ain't got no alternative but to let you go. No, mister, I don't intend to kill you just yet, an' none of these folk would ever have the nerve to kill you in cold blood. Now get goin' before I change my mind. Before you go though, maybe you can answer me one question. What the hell is so damned important about this particular piece of land that makes Brindley want it so much?'

'I'm just a hired hand, McNally,' replied the man. 'Mr Brindley don't confide in the likes of me.'

'You must hear things,' prompted Brogan. 'Hired hands hear a lot of what's goin' on.'

'Like I say, I'm just the hired help,' came the reply. 'It don't do to know about too many things what don't concern a man, especially where James Brindley is concerned. I seen him kill a man just because he thought he was listenin' in on a conversation he was havin'. No other reason at all. That's the kind of man he is. He's a worse killer than any man he hires.'

'OK,' said Brogan. 'Just get the hell

out of here while you still can.' The man stooped to retrieve his gun but Brogan stepped on the man's hand and slowly eased the gun from his grasp. 'I don't think so,' he said. 'If you want it back I suggest you ask Mr Brindley to come and ask for it. If he asks nice enough an' promises to leave these good folk alone, I just might give it back to you. You can tell him I said so as well.'

'Go eat shit an' rot in hell, McNally,' snarled the man.

'I most probably will rot in hell,' said Brogan. 'Most preachers reckon that's where I'm headed an' I suppose they ought to know. I don't mind though, they say it'll be warm down there an' I hate the cold. I've eaten some mighty strange things in my time as well but I don't eat shit. In the meantime this gun might come in handy for shootin' at hired hands what come lookin' for trouble. You won't be needin' that gunbelt, either. Drop it an' get the hell out of here.'

The man dropped his gunbelt, which

contained about twelve bullets, snarled something which sounded obscene and which most certainly questioned Brogan's parentage. It was an observation with which Brogan was forced to agree, replying that it was a very wise man who knew his own father.

When he had gone, Brogan ushered the boys back to the village where, to save them from punishment by their fathers, he announced that Pablo and Miguel had saved his life. At least that much was true, they probably had.

The boys swaggered around the village soaking up the adulation of the other children. Inevitably their exploits had already assumed epic proportions in their young minds and became more wondrous with each telling.

'There was a rifle with one of the horses,' announced Jose. 'There are bullets also. Some are for the rifle but I think others for the pistols.'

'I'll sort 'em out,' said Brogan. 'Have you all decided what you are going to do about Brindley?'

'It has been decided that those who wish to leave can do so,' said Jose. 'There are a few who are saying they are leaving but most are prepared to stay and fight. There is but one condition for this.'

'Condition?' queried Brogan. 'I don't think you quite get the idea. You're in no position to make conditions of any kind. Brindley and his men are likely to be here any moment now. I don't reckon nobody's got time to leave even if they want to. Just what the hell is this condition?'

'The condition is that you lead us in this fight,' said Jose. 'We might be willing but we do not have experience.'

'And I do?'

'Sí, Señor McNally,' answered Jose. 'We have been talking and we believe that you are very experienced.'

'I guess I've learnt a thing or two over the years,' agreed Brogan. 'Well, I guess that's the least I can do. Anyhow, I already signed my death warrant as far as Brindley is concerned so I might as well go down fightin'. Right, first thing we do is send somebody out to keep an eye open for Brindley an' his men.' He called Pablo and Miguel over. 'I got a job that'll be just perfect for two bright boys like you,' he said. 'You get your little asses out along the road there an' let me know the moment you see anybody headin' this way.'

'*Sí, sí*, Señor Brogan,' said Miguel. 'Me and Pablo we know just the place from where to see anyone coming.'

'I thought you might,' said Brogan. 'Now, get goin'.'

He watched the two boys race through the ford and disappear. He stood in the middle of the road leading to the river and surveyed the village. It was obvious to him that the river itself would have to form part of their defences. It was not deep, especially across the ford but it was a natural barrier. There were no buildings close to the river and no large rocks or boulders behind which men could hide, but there were several small trees.

'Have you any men who can use the guns you have?' he asked Jose as he examined the guns and ammunition they had acquired. 'I think you might even have to bring some of them old pieces you got into action as well. They won't be a lot of use, really, but even a single ball-shot might cause a few problems.'

'Sí,' replied Jose. 'I myself have used a pistol and I think there is a younger man who can use a rifle. I will ask if there is anyone else. As for the old rifles and pistols, they are so old I do not believe there is anyone who even knows how to load them. Besides, I do not think we have the ammunition and I am certain nobody has any gunpowder.'

'I figured that might be the case,' said Brogan. 'So, we've got three pistols an' one rifle an' about twenty rounds for each, that's in addition to mine.' He gave a deep sigh. 'I can't say as it's a lot to work on. You'll probably waste far more bullets than you use effectively.'

At that moment Maria appeared. She

seemed none the worse for her ordeal. In fact she was smiling broadly.

'Señor Brogan,' she said. 'I have been tending Señor Callista, he is very ill and near death. He has no family now except for a cousin in another village far away. I think there is something about which you ought to know. I do not think anyone else in the village knows of it.'

'What's that, Maria?' asked Brogan. 'Unless you found an unknown armoury I don't think it's goin' to be much use.'

'An armoury, no, *señor*,' she replied. '*Dynamite, sí.*'

'Dynamite!' exclaimed Brogan. 'Dynamite! Are you sure.'

'I think so, *señor*,' she said. 'I have seen it with my own eyes and I also read English pretty good. The name on the boxes is most definitely *dynamite*. Inside there are brown sticks which I think is dynamite.'

'Maria, I love you!' Brogan exclaimed, grasping her shoulders and kissing her forehead. 'Lead me to it.'

'You make me blush, Señor Brogan,' she said. 'No man has ever told me he loves me.'

'Don't get the wrong idea, Maria,' he said. 'It was just what we call a figure of speech. It don't really mean anythin'.'

'Sí, I know this,' she said with a slightly sad expression in her eyes. 'Anyway, you are far too old for me.'

'I ain't that old,' complained Brogan.

She gave him a broad smile and led him and Jose to an adobe where there was an old man lying on a straw filled palliasse. He hardly appeared to notice them as they entered the room, being far more interested in a picture he was clutching. The palliasse was raised off the floor by what appeared to be an ancient iron bedstead. Maria lifted the side of a dirty blanket which hid most of the frame. There were a lot of boxes and parcels.

'There are many boxes,' she said. 'Most are filled with nothing except his belongings and are worth nothing to anyone. He had asked me to find an old picture of his wife. He had it painted when they were first married. She died many years ago. He told me it was in a box under his bed. I found the picture but I also found two boxes at the back against the wall. The one had a loose lid so when I saw the name, I looked inside. I know I should not have looked, but it was well, perhaps, that I did.' She indicated two small wooden boxes at the back.

Brogan dragged the boxes out and lifted the lid of one of them. Inside he found eight sticks of what was most definitely dynamite. They appeared to be rather old and were not in the best of condition. He prised the lid off the other box and found that it contained another twelve sticks in the same unstable condition. He picked up one of them and examined it more closely.

'Seems a mite on the wet side' he said, pointing out to Jose some nitro-glycerine weeping from a joint. 'It should still be OK though, just needs handlin' carefully. I wonder just how long it's been under his bed? The state it's in he could've easily blown up himself an' a few of his neighbours. There's enough here to flatten half the village.'

Maria spoke to the man but he simply ignored her. Jose seemed very wary of the dynamite.

'I have seen men killed by this,' he explained to Brogan. 'It was not a pretty sight. I do not trust it.'

'It's fine as long as you know what you're doin',' Brogan assured him. 'If it bothers you though, you might as well leave now. It don't do to have a nervous man handlin' this stuff.'

'*Sí*, I will leave,' said Jose. 'Maria, you must come too.'

'I will be fine, Uncle Jose,' she said. 'I am not afraid.'

'No, you probably handled it before as well,' muttered Brogan.

'Oh, no, *señor*,' she said. 'I have never even seen any before in my life.' She smiled at her uncle. 'Do not worry, Uncle Jose, I shall be all right. Señor

Brogan he will look after me.'

Jose muttered something beneath his breath and left the adobe. When he had gone Brogan looked at Maria and smiled.

'Don't nothin' scare you?' he asked.

'Only bats, señor,' she said with a cheeky grin. 'You know, flying mice. I am very frightened of bats. They can become tangled in your hair and they suck your blood when you are asleep.' She looked down at the old man. 'He does not have much longer to live, Señor Brogan,' she said. 'Death I have seen many times. In Los Cahuillas we have all seen death. It is unavoidable. He is the oldest man in the village and it is said that he is well over eighty years old. My uncle Jose or Señor Gramali could tell you more about him if you want to know.'

'No, it ain't that important,' said Brogan. 'Now, I don't want nobody messin' with this stuff, it ain't too safe. I'm goin' to take it across to the church, I reckon that's just about the safest place for it.'

'I can help?' asked Maria.

'No, I don't want nobody touchin' it, especially you,' insisted Brogan. 'I didn't risk my life savin' you from those men just for you to blow yourself up. I'll manage it on my own.'

He picked up the full box of twelve and gingerly carried it to the church. By that time word had circulated about what had been discovered and the village square was full of curious but silent people. Brogan thought about ordering them away but decided that it was hardly worth while. He did, however, call the headman, Gramali, over.

'Just make it plain to your people that this stuff is very dangerous,' he said. 'I don't want nobody, nobody at all, you understand, to go anywhere near it unless I say it's OK.'

'*Sí, señor*,' said Gramali. 'I understand. Seve Callista, he always used to boast that he had dynamite but nobody ever believed him. He was an old man but when he was younger he was always telling stories which nobody ever believed. He was from another village but married a woman from here. He said that he had been in the army, but we know this was not true.'

'Well, he sure got it from somewhere,' said Brogan. 'The army would be a good bet as well.'

At that moment Brogan had no idea at all how exactly he was going to use the dynamite. All he knew was that in the past he had used it to great effect. The important thing now was to look around and work out a strategy.

When he eventually left the church Brogan was faced by four men, including Jose. The other three were probably in their twenties.

'I think these men can use guns, señor,' said Jose. 'I do know Manolo here can use a rifle. His father before him could use one and was the only man in the village to own one. He taught Manolo how to use it.'

'You don't have the rifle now?' asked Brogan.

'No, *señor*,' said Manolo. 'My father he lost it when he went hunting one day. At least that is what he claimed but my mother and me we thought that he had sold it. At the time we had no money.'

'Well, you sure can't eat bullets,' admitted Brogan. 'OK, let me see you shoot.' He looked about for a target. He eventually decided on a small rock which had been placed on top of a wall about thirty yards away. 'See if you can hit that rock,' he instructed.

Manolo slowly raised the rifle and took careful aim. He fired and the bullet plainly ricocheted off its target. He lowered the rifle looking quite pleased with himself. Brogan, however, did not seem at all happy. He snatched the rifle, stood with his back to the target and suddenly turned, at the same time crouching, and fired. This time the rock definitely moved.

'You gotta learn to move an' shoot at the same time,' said Brogan. 'You ain't always goin' to have the time to take a good aim. Any average gunman would kill you long before that.'

'I hope I shall not be out in the open, Señor McNally,' said Manolo. 'I will be shooting from cover.'

'Probably,' agreed Brogan. He gave a deep sigh. 'OK, maybe I'm expectin' too much. You're goin' to be a very important part of anythin' what happens. You will be shootin' at a target from a distance, just make sure you hit it.' He looked at the slightly worried expression on Manolo's face for a moment and smiled. 'Reckon you could kill a man?' he asked. 'It sounds easy an' looks easy but believe me it just ain't that easy for a beginner.'

'I have killed a deer and I have killed wolves,' replied Manolo. 'The wolves I found easy to kill, they were attacking my sheep and goats.'

'Then the best thing you can do is start thinkin' about Brindley an' his men as wolves,' advised Brogan.

Jose brought another young man forward. 'This is Stephan,' he introduced.

'He claims to have fired a pistol before.'

'How often?' asked Brogan.

'Three times only,' replied Stephan. 'My uncle, he live in another village, he allow me to fire a pistol he owned.'

'Did you hit anythin'?' asked Brogan.

'Hit anything? No, *señor*,' admitted Stephan. 'I was not trying to hit anything. There was nothing to shoot at as I remember.'

'As you remember?' queried Brogan. 'How long ago was this?'

'I was ten years old,' admitted Stephan.

'Bloody hell!' Brogan muttered to himself. 'OK let's see you try to hit that rock over there.' He pointed to the same rock as before.

Stephan raised the gun, sighted along the barrel and fired. The recoil made his arm jerk up in the air and the bullet could have gone anywhere. He immediately lowered his arm again, grasped the gun with both hands and, before Brogan could prevent him, fired again. This time he succeeded in hitting the wall below and about three feet to the right of the target.

'You learn fast,' Brogan grudgingly admitted. 'There's four more bullets, let's see you get a bit closer to the rock.'

Stephan's third shot once again hit the wall below and to the right of his target. He looked at the gun as though it was at fault and not he before taking aim for a fourth time. This time, although still below the target, it was at least in line. For some strange reason his fifth shot went well wide but the sixth and final shot once again hit the wall in line but below the target. This time it was, however, a little higher.

'You'd probably've hit him in his balls,' said Brogan with a broad grin. 'Wouldn't've killed him but it sure would've made him yell an' put him out of action. OK, son, you'll do just fine. Remember what you did just now an' make sure you don't miss if you have to. Reckon you can kill a man?'

'I have never killed anything but sheep or goats,' admitted Stephan. 'I know I can slit the throat of the goat and think nothing of it. I think shooting a man it will be easier than catching the goat and slitting its throat. *Sí*, Señor McNally, I think I can do this. I would not choose to do it but I will if I have to.'

'Yeah, I reckon you will too,' said Brogan.

He looked at the third man. Immediately he had very serious doubts about him. He was not very tall, was extremely thin and even appeared slightly deformed in his hands. He looked as though a strong wind would blow him away. Brogan looked at Jose questioningly. Jose smiled and handed the man a gun.

'With this one I think you will be very surprised,' said Jose. 'His name is Pedro. He speaks no English. I will translate.'

Brogan smiled and pointed at the rock. Pedro needed nobody to translate as he suddenly and surprisingly quickly raised the gun and fired without seeming to take aim. The bullet struck the wall immediately adjacent to the stone. He grunted and immediately fired again. This time the bullet hit the stone full on. Jose had been quite right, Brogan was very surprised and quite impressed. The man had plainly used a handgun before.

'Where'd you learn to shoot like that?' he asked. Jose translated.

'He says he is a deserter from the Mexican army,' he told Brogan. 'Until now I did not know this. He came to our village only one year ago. He came with his wife and small son. His wife's uncle, he lives in the village and her mother was from here, although she is now dead.'

'Welcome,' said Brogan extending his hand. 'Ain't no need to ask you to shoot again.' Pedro smiled and shook Brogan's hand. 'OK,' Brogan said to them all. 'I reckon there ain't no need to tell you you is liable to get yourselves killed. Are you sure you want to go through with it?' He spoke to Pedro and Jose translated. 'You got a wife an' son to think about.'

'He says this was the idea of his wife,' said Jose. 'She knows what might happen.'

'OK,' said Brogan. 'All we got to do now is put you somewhere where you can do the most damage an' where they won't get at you too easy. Pity there ain't more cover round here.'

For the next half-hour Brogan took all the men round the village, deciding and showing them where they were to go if and when the shooting started. He placed Manolo in the church bell-tower, which meant that he had a good view of most of the village. Being there also meant that Manolo could take his time and aim a bit more. Stephan he placed behind an old wagon at the end of a group of three adobes and Jose was placed in a narrow alley between two adobes but looking towards the river and the village square.

'Pedro,' he said to the deserter, 'you an' me we go where we're needed.' Jose translated. 'Best thing you can do is keep moving,' advised Brogan.

Pedro grinned and nodded. He replied in Spanish.

'He says that he deserted because he does not like fighting and slaughtering innocent peons,' said Jose. 'but in this case he believes it to be a just fight.'

'Only hope he's right,' said Brogan.

Having sorted out his guns Brogan turned his attention back to the dynamite. In actual fact there was nowhere for it to be placed where it would cause any real damage or problems to Brindley.

Apart from a few trees down by the river and a solitary thorn tree in the village square, there was nothing which could be blown up and the land around was very flat. There were a few large boulders on the opposite side of the river but nothing very close. He eventually decided that the dynamite could only be effectively used as a diversion.

'OK, I guess there ain't much more

we can do but wait,' said Brogan. 'Jose, go find Miguel Gramali an' get him to make sure that everybody who ain't fightin' is well hid. I don't want nobody catchin' a stray bullet. The shootin' is likely to start any time now so I'd like for the village to be clear before they gets here. It'd be better if everybody went out of the village.'

'Miguel is a good man,' said Jose, 'but I think he does not like what we do. I think he believes we will all be slaughtered.'

'Chances are you'll all be slaughtered anyhow,' said Brogan. 'Choice is yours, not mine. Say the word an' I'll get the hell out of it right now.'

'He might be the head of this village but he does not have the power to decide what we do,' said Jose. 'Only the council of village elders can do this.'

'And what do the elders think?' asked Brogan. 'Not that it's goin' to make that much difference at this stage of things.'

'They all agree with me,' said Jose. 'We stand against Brindley.'

'Good,' said Brogan. 'Now, where the hell is Brindley? I expected him here before now. I only hope them two boys is all right.'

'The boys, they will be fine,' assured Jose. 'They know this country very well. They will see him come long before he gets here.'

'In the meantime I think a drink of your beer would go down very nicely,' said Brogan. 'Dyin' is thirsty work.'

5

It seemed a very long time before the two boys came racing back, calling out at the tops of their voices. Brogan came out to meet them, having heard them long before they even reached the ford. Jose and the other men joined him.

'OK, boys,' he said as the boys slid to a halt in the village square, 'I think we all get the message. How far away are they and could you tell how many of them there are?'

'*Sí, sí*,' came the panted reply from Miguel. 'They do not travel fast but they come. I think there are six of them, perhaps seven, but no more. They should be here very soon now.'

'Jose,' Brogan ordered, 'you all know what to do now, get yourselves in position. Just remember, don't shoot until you have to. You'll know when I guess. It should be obvious.'

'*Sí*,' replied Jose. 'What will you do?'

'Meet 'em at the ford,' said Brogan. He was joined by the ex-soldier, Pedro. 'Pedro,' said Brogan, 'you keep out of sight but keep me covered. There's a couple of trees you can use as cover.' He pointed to the trees. Pedro apparently did not need anyone to translate, as he nodded and ran towards the river. 'Manolo,' he called up to the man climbing into the bell-tower. 'You take good aim but don't shoot until I give you a signal or if they start first. Make sure your target is Brindley himself. You got that?' Manolo raised his hand to acknowledge that he understood.

Brogan ordered the two boys to run and hide, although he had the feeling that they would not be able to resist watching. However, there was nothing he could do to stop them at that moment. He only hoped that they would not do anything stupid. He looked around the village and was satisfied that everything was in order before strolling towards the ford, where he waited for James Brindley to arrive. He did not have to wait too long.

Seven horses and riders came to a halt in a line just short of the ford and for a few moments they simply stared at Brogan. He was slightly surprised that none of them attempted to use his gun but reasoned that it was because he already held his. He had his rifle in one hand and his Colt in the other.

Eventually Brindley moved forward to the water's edge, drew his rifle from the saddle holster with a flourish but not making any obvious attempt to shoot, and rested the butt on his thigh. He looked at Brogan and sneered.

'On your own, McNally?' he asked as he looked about. His sneer turned to a knowing smile and he nodded. 'No, somehow I don't reckon you are. You ain't that stupid. That's the only reason I told my men not to shoot and why you're still standing there. I don't like it when a man like you almost invites somebody to kill him. I'm surprised they're backing you up, I didn't think any of them had the guts to stand up to me.'

'Right now there's four guns aimed at your guts,' said Brogan. 'You'd be the first they'd shoot. This is as far as you go, Brindley.'

'*Mister* Brindley, if you don't mind,' sneered Brindley. 'You should always treat your betters with respect, McNally.'

'Then maybe you'd better call me *Mister* McNally,' said Brogan. 'It looks like I've got the better of you right now.'

'OK, have it your way.' Brindley sneered again. 'You can have your moment of glory, I don't mind. So, you've got four guns in addition to your own. I don't know if they know how to use those guns but I have to assume they do. Sure, it makes sense you've got more guns, you took them off my men. I see you've got a rifle and a pistol but, I ask myself, can you use both at once? No, don't answer that, I reckon you just might be able to. There's seven of us, *Mister* McNally and if I know these people, at this precise moment even the four you've persuaded to fight will all be so damned scared they'll be shittin' their pants. You might have given them guns but I don't think there's one of them who knows how to handle one properly. You've probably shown them a few things but they can't have learned much in such a short time. Maybe I'm wrong, but I don't think so.'

'Well there's one sure way to find out, *Mister* Brindley,' invited Brogan. 'All you got to do is cross the river.'

'And you'll be dead the moment we do,' Brindley assured him.

'Maybe so, maybe not,' said Brogan. 'Thing is, so will at least four of you. The question is, which four? How about you, Brindley, do you fancy bein' one of 'em? If we're both dead it'll make all of this a waste of time. How about you, Jake?' he said to the man alongside Brindley. 'You got away last time, reckon your luck will hold out this time?' Jake moved slightly in his saddle, a movement which told Brogan that he was very nervous.

'You're bluffing, McNally,' said Brindley, although his voice was a little hoarse which again told Brogan that he too was nervous.

'Could be,' replied Brogan with a broad grin. 'I ain't much of a poker-player but I have played a few times. Strange thing is, I always won an' I still ain't sure if I was bluffin' or not. Thing is, I like to bet on a sure-fire certainty. Do you play poker, *Mister* Brindley? They do say a good poker-player can always tell when a man's bluffin' but nobody ever knows when *he's* bluffin'. Are you a *good* poker-player, Brindley? It's up to you, it's fine with me, you can call my bluff if'n that's the way you want to play it.'

'Just remind me never to play poker with you,' said Brindley with a dry and slightly nervous laugh. The nervousness was not lost on Brogan. 'But,' Brindley continued, 'I'd say the hand you're holding consists of one ace — you. All the other cards in your hand count for nothing.'

'You could be right at that,' agreed Brogan. 'Thing is though, *Mister* Brindley this ain't no game of poker. All you is likely to lose playin' poker is a few dollars. Call my bluff now an' you could just as easy end up dead. All I will tell you is that all four of those guns are aimed at your belly. Sure, you might be able to kill me but are you prepared to chance just one of them four bullets rippin' your innards out or makin' a hole in your head?'

Jake whispered to Brindley and both men looked up at the church tower.

'I see you have a man in the bell-tower,' said Brindley. 'That means he must have a rifle. We know there was one. That probably means that the other three must have pistols and since they are not too close, I'd say they most likely wouldn't do a lot of damage.'

'Could be,' agreed Brogan, 'but you'll never really know unless you try callin' my bluff. Choice is yours, Brindley.'

Brindley suddenly laughed out loud. '*Mister* McNally,' he said, 'I certainly have to hand it to you. You do not seem to be scared of anything or anyone. You don't even seem that bothered about dying.'

'We all got to die sometime,' said Brogan. 'Nobody wants to die but when you're dead you ain't got no more problems.'

'Very true,' agreed Brindley. 'Like I say, I have to take my hat off to you.' He reached up to remove his hat but Brogan stopped him.

'I don't fall for that old trick, Brindley,' he said. 'The moment that hat leaves your head you is a dead man.'

Brindley's hand grasped the brim of his hat but he did not remove it. 'There's a saying about teaching old dogs new tricks,' he said, giving Brogan a broad smile. 'I reckon you're a very old dog but you already know all the tricks. Very well, *Mister* McNally, on this occasion I am forced to admit we've reached something of a stalemate and I shall return to my ranch. The chances are that I could take this village here and now but I give you a certain amount of credit for knowing what you are doing. There's just too much doubt on my part and I do not take any risks at all. I don't play poker either. It's a pity, I could use a man like you. That will not be the end of the matter though. Rest assured, this village will be mine before very long no matter what you do.'

'Talkin' of this village,' said Brogan. 'Just what the hell is so damned important about it?'

'Let's just say it's very important,' replied Brindley. 'By the way, you are now living on borrowed time, McNally. This village will be mine. You stay and you will never leave here alive. I hope I make myself understood.'

'Yeah, I heard it all before,' said Brogan, rather boastfully. 'If'n I had me a dollar for every time I been told that or somethin' very similar, I'd be a rich man now. Thing is, I'm still around an' most of them what threatened me ain't.'

'I can see that,' said Brindley with

another broad smile. He reached up for his hat again but this time he raised it clear of his head, nodded at Brogan and grinned again. He replaced his hat. 'Until we meet again, *Mister* McNally,' he continued. 'Oh, and if you change your mind or have a change of heart, I am still willing to take you on and forget all about what happened here.'

'I don't reckon so,' said Brogan. 'I have worked for my livin' on the odd occasion, but that ain't been too often. When I do though, I'm very particular who I work for. I like to keep things all legal.'

'Of course,' said Brindley. 'I somehow wouldn't expect otherwise. The invitation still stands though. I bid you farewell for the moment, McNally. I shall be back, and very soon.'

Brindley turned his horse and galloped off. His men followed although Jake did say something as he turned which even Brogan's sharp ears could not fully make out. He had little doubt from the odd word he did hear properly that it was bringing his parentage into question once again.

Jose joined Brogan at the river and Brogan could see that he was shaking. Stephan and Pedro on the other hand appeared perfectly composed. Manolo had remained in the tower, apparently making quite certain that Brindley and his men were well clear.

'Have you ever done anythin' like this before?' Brogan asked Jose. 'The way you're shakin' tells me you haven't.'

'It is that obvious?' asked Jose. 'No, Señor McNally, I have never been in such a situation before. I do not mind telling you I was really frightened.'

'I too was scared,' said Stephan. 'I do not know how you were able to face Brindley as you did.'

'Somebody had to,' replied Brogan, actually enjoying being cast as the brave man. 'I guess you weren't scared,' he said to Pedro. Jose translated.

'*Sí*,' said Jose. 'He was not scared. But that was because it was not him facing those men. He was more scared when his troop faced some renegade Apache Indians and the Indians were outnumbered and presented no real danger. He does not trust any Indians.'

'Indians ain't no worse an' no better than nobody else,' said Brogan. 'OK, I guess you all know what they said an' I don't think Brindley was bluffin'. They'll be back, nothin' more certain.'

'*Sí*,' said Jose. 'The question is when.'

Suddenly Stephan pointed up the river. Miguel and Pablo, the two boys, were crossing. Brogan called out but the boys simply ignored him. They soon disappeared amongst the bushes.

'I guess they'll tell us when,' said Brogan. 'Come on, Jose, like I said before, this gettin' ready to die is thirsty work. I need a beer.'

★ ★ ★

It was late afternoon when the two boys eventually reappeared and, as they probably expected, they each received a telling-off from their respective parents.

However, this did not seem to make much impression on them. They found Brogan and Miguel blurted out what they had seen.

'I do not understand what Señor Brindley is doing,' said Miguel. 'His men are collecting cattle together. So far they must have rounded up perhaps two hundred of them.'

'Cows!' exclaimed Brogan. 'I thought he had other things on his mind. How far away are they?'

'On the other side of the big hill,' said Miguel. 'The hill with a single pine-tree at the top of it.'

'I seen it,' said Brogan. 'Does he normally keep cattle there?'

'He sometimes keeps a few there,' said Miguel, 'but I have never seen as many as he now gathers together.'

'Then all I can say is there must be a reason for it,' said Brogan. 'A man like Brindley has a reason for everythin' he does.'

In the meantime the other boy, Pablo, had been telling those villagers who did not speak English what they had seen.

'Señor McNally,' Pedro, the ex-soldier said to Brogan. He then spoke in Spanish, which Brogan did not understand at all.

'What the hell's he sayin'?' Brogan asked. This time it was young Miguel who translated.

'He say he think Señor Brindley is going to do what he once did when he was in the army,' said Miguel. He waited for Pedro to say more. 'He say he think Señor Brindley is going to drive the cattle through the village. Even if the cows they do no damage, that is not the purpose, the men will use them as cover to ride into the village.'

'That sure makes sense,' admitted Brogan. 'I've seen the same sorta thing happen with horses.'

'It will be impossible to stop that many cows,' said Jose. 'Those men, they will be able to get into the village very easily. If they do we will easily be defeated and I fear they will slaughter everybody.'

'Well we can't just sit here waitin' for it to happen,' said Brogan. 'Miguel, I want you two to take me as close to the cattle as possible.'

'*Sí, sí,* Señor, McNally,' said Miguel, giving his father a broad, cheeky and almost triumphant smile. 'It is not problem. We get very close.'

'Well, let's go take a look while there's still some daylight,' said Brogan. 'We ain't got no time to waste.'

He followed the boys across the ford and along the road for about half a mile. Then Miguel motioned for him to keep out of sight. The road narrowed quite sharply between two hills, the one with the single pine-tree on top to the left and a smaller hill to the right. The pass between the two was quite narrow — no more than forty feet — but not very long — no more than fifty yards. The sides were almost sheer and rose more than 200 feet. Once through Brogan was looking

115

down on a large herd of cattle.

It appeared to him that the men were preparing to stay for the night as they were in the process of lighting two fires. One was plainly a cooking-fire, since it already had a pot on it.

Brogan studied the scene for a few minutes before motioning for the boys to return to the village. However, Brogan did not hurry back. He spent some considerable length of time studying the small pass and its rocks. He and the boys eventually arrived back in the village just as darkness closed in.

'It sure looks like Pedro was right,' Brogan said to Jose. 'There just ain't no other reason for collectin' that many cows together. I'd say they intend comin' through first thing in the mornin'.'

'I have been talking to Miguel, the headman,' said Jose. 'Already a few are leaving. They fear that to stay will mean only death for everyone. He is leading those who wish to leave now. They are mainly the old and the women with small children and few others. Most of the younger men they stay.'

'It might be better if there was nobody in the village who don't have a gun,' said Brogan. 'Stayin' here ain't goin' to help none.'

Jose laughed. 'I think you do not understand the Mexican mind, señor,' he said. 'Most gringos consider us to be weak and afraid and in many ways perhaps they are right, we are not fighting people. Guns we do not have. However, that does not mean that we always run away. There are three things which we all hold very dear. The first is our family. The family is the most important thing. We will do almost anything to protect our family. The second is our land. We work hard, we are farmers. The third thing is, of course, our church. Normally we would do what our priest tells us to do but we have no priest. But Father Alonso, he said that this land was worth fighting for. For this reason many are prepared to stay and fight with our bare hands if we have to.'

'You just might end up doin' that,' said Brogan. 'Anyhow, I don't think they're goin' to do anythin' until first light. That gives me all night to think of somethin' to stop 'em. In fact I got me an idea.'

'You wish for some help?' asked Jose.

'No, I don't think so,' said Brogan. 'Don't bother lookin' for me, I probably won't be around. You an' the others be in position at first light, just in case. Oh, an' try to make sure them boys keep well out of the way. I don't want 'em gettin' killed or injured.'

'I will see to them personally,' assured Jose. 'If it is necessary I shall tie them up and lock them away.'

★ ★ ★

It turned out to be one of those nights which had no moon. Apart from the glimmer of stars there was no light at all. Brogan made his way towards the pass using nothing but his normally unerring sense of direction, although in truth even a blind man could have found the way.

Although Jose had tried to question him about his plans, Brogan had insisted that he did not have any. This was actually true, all he had was a general idea but no specific plan. The only thing he did have and about which he had not told Jose, was that he now carried a box of dynamite and a tinder-box. His idea was quite simple; he intended to block the pass.

He had to admit that it was really nothing more than a gesture. He had no doubt that there were other ways round and that at best it would delay Brindley for perhaps another day, but not much longer. However, even one more day was a breathing-space during which time he could come up with other ideas.

He was approaching the pass; he could just make out the tops of the two hills against the light of the stars and he sensed rather than saw the steep walls of the pass. Suddenly his senses were screaming at him and he never ignored his senses. He stopped and hid behind a large rock where he listened and watched.

Listening was about the only sense which was of any use at that moment. Although his eyes had long since grown accustomed to the dark, there was very little to see until he was almost on top of it. However, this did not bother him, it would be exactly the same for anyone else and it was unlikely that they were as conditioned to such things as he was.

What had alerted him he did not really know: that was often the case, but it was most probably a sound. His ears did not need that much sound to alert him, it was one of his proud boasts that he could hear a fly land on a piece of dung from fifty yards. Plainly this was an exaggeration but his hearing was very acute and had saved his life on many occasions. He waited and listened.

At first there was nothing else to be

heard but even so he did not dismiss his instinct. If there was anything or anyone there he would hear it again. It was, of course, quite possible that the sound had been made by an animal. There were probably deer, foxes, rabbits and even wolves or mountain lions about, but somehow he thought it most unlikely that there would be any around just there at that moment.

This feeling was based on nothing more than his knowledge of the habits and movements of such animals. There were men around not too far away and most animals tended to avoid men. The presence of cattle would not bother them but the sound and smell of men would.

He stiffened slightly as he heard the sound again. The difference was that this time it was most definitely a voice. In fact it proved to be two voices: two men were heading through the pass in his direction.

He guessed that they had stopped. They certainly did not seem to be in any hurry but eventually their voices became clearer. They were getting closer but he still could not actually see them.

Dealing with whomsoever it was really presented Brogan with few problems. He knew that he could quite easily handle them, even in the dark. Surprise was on his side and he was expert at surprise stealth attacks. His problem was that he wondered if it was worth the bother. They would undoubtedly be missed and a search instituted. That in turn could well lead to the discovery of any dynamite charges he had laid. He decided against taking the men out.

The two men walked very slowly and even stood right next to the rock behind which he was hiding. Had one of them reached out he might even have touched him. The men moved away and eventually made their way back towards their camp. Brogan moved out to make certain that they were heading back and discovered that they and two other men were camped only a few yards from the pass. They had lit a small fire which Brogan had not seen because it was behind what seemed to be the stump of a tree.

This discovery complicated matters somewhat but even so he was quite confident that he would be able to lay his dynamite without being seen or heard. He positioned himself behind another rock, this time looking down on to the four men no more than ten yards away.

There was no point in laying the dynamite and returning to the village, and that had not been his intention; he needed to be there to light each fuse. Each one needed to be lit individually since he had no fuse to connect them. He decided to wait until the men were asleep before making his move.

He thought it was probably about four o'clock when he started looking for holes and cracks in which to place his dynamite. In actual fact the sky had taken on a slightly lighter tone as the first rays of dawn were breaking in the east. Even so, it was still very dark.

He checked on the four men and decided that they were asleep. Their fire was still alight, although now consisting mainly of charred embers. He decided that if possible he would use one of the hot sticks to light his fuses. It would be a lot quicker and easier than using the tinder-box.

Placing the dynamite was really quite easy and before very long he had placed six sticks. He reasoned that six would be enough to create the damage and diversion he was looking for.

He remembered exactly where he had placed the first two, one either side of the entrance to the pass. Although he had a pretty good idea where the other four were, he might easily miss them should anything happen before it was daylight. He had to hope that Brindley's men were not early risers. The first real light of dawn found Brogan behind a rock no more than ten yards from the four men and alongside one of his sticks of dynamite.

With dawn the cows became rather more vocal. Brogan could see their breath in the early morning coldness and the noise of the cattle seemed to be a signal for the men to wake up at the other camp-fires as well. The four nearest Brogan stood up, went through the habitual scratch and yawn which Brogan himself indulged in and then relieved themselves. One of them kicked some earth on to the fire and they picked up their saddles and bedrolls. Their horses were with others tethered some distance down the hill. Brogan waited for them to reach the horses before moving.

He had cursed the man who had kicked dirt over the fire but it was a habit which the vast majority of travelling men had. It was purely that, a habit. He did, however, manage to find one piece of wood which, when he blew on the end, glowed brightly . . .

6

Judging by the number of horses tethered, it appeared that James Brindley could call on no more than nine men. Brogan had faced worse odds, but not very often. However, this total did not seem to include James Brindley himself, as he suddenly appeared already on horseback, calling his men to him.

Brogan could make out odd words but little else and it really was not very important. Eventually the men mounted their horses and dispersed in all directions. It was obvious that they were herding the cattle together. This activity made the animals more restless and soon the air was filled with noise and dust.

Two riders made their way towards the pass; obviously their job was to prevent cows dispersing too far once they were through. This left Brogan with no choice, he had to act.

He blew on the charred ember, managed to create a glow and lit the fuse of the first stick of dynamite. Knowing that he was almost certain to be seen, he then ran across to the other side of the pass.

Inevitably he was seen and a bullet raised dust a few feet away but that single shot had told him that he was, for the moment, out of range. He also knew that in a matter of seconds he would be within range as both men spurred their horses into a gallop. They were still some forty or fifty yards away when the second charge was lit and he ran down to the third.

The two men were plainly very wary and reined their horses to a halt some distance away from Brogan. He breathed a sigh of relief, at least it gave him some further time and space.

By that time the cattle were on the move and heading towards the pass. The actions and shouting of the two men as they attempted to warn the others could not prevent this mass movement and in any case nobody seemed to see or hear the men calling.

The two riders suddenly raced forward, both shooting at Brogan. This time they were much closer to Brogan and he now knew for certain that he was within range. The third stick of dynamite was rather more difficult to light, but eventually it was lit and he dashed across to the fourth.

The two riders were now very close and another bullet ricocheted off a rock dangerously near to Brogan's head. This forced him to duck but he managed to light the dynamite and race off down the pass. A few bullets raised dust close behind him but it seemed that the men were not too anxious to continue the chase.

Suddenly and almost unexpectedly, although it should not have been so to Brogan at least, there was a loud explosion and the whole area was showered with debris. What happened to the two men Brogan did not notice but a few seconds later the second charge erupted. This was closely followed by the third explosion, then the fourth and Brogan ducked behind a large boulder for protection. He regretted not being able to light the other two charges but it appeared that the four he had lit had blown a lot of rock.

When things had settled he found his horse and looked back, his gun in his hand just in case of trouble, but there was no sign of the men. He could hear the loud calling of cows obviously terrified by the explosions, but they seemed to be some distance away and he assumed and hoped that the explosions had stampeded the animals in the opposite direction.

He waited for some time but there was no movement along the pass and he reasoned that his plan must have worked. However, just to be certain, he slowly made his way back along the now debris-strewn track.

There was no doubt about it, the

head of the pass was now effectively blocked. A cautious look over the pile of rocks showed that the cattle were now well dispersed but still stampeding away from the pass.

He saw several men who appeared to be gathering together but he could not see Brindley. Whether or not the two men sent through the pass were still alive Brogan neither knew nor cared. He was satisfied that it was now impossible to drive the cattle through.

★   ★   ★

He was greeted at Los Cahuillas by very curious villagers. It seemed that all had heard the explosions and speculation abounded as to what had occurred. It was actually Maria who had explained what she thought had happened, since she had found that the dynamite was missing. Brogan himself did not explain in any great detail, he simply confirmed that he had blocked the pass and that the danger of cattle stampeding through the village was, for the moment, averted.

'Can they get round?' Brogan asked Jose.

'Sí,' replied Jose, 'it is possible, but it is a long way and cows they do not move very quickly. I do not think that Brindley will try again. He must know what we might expect.'

'Probably not,' agreed Brogan. 'He's lost the element of surprise now. All we can do is wait and see what he does next. He won't take this lyin' down, that's for sure.'

'I think all he can do now is a direct attack,' said Jose. 'Even with your help, señor, I do not believe we will survive such an attack. We do not have the men or the guns.'

'You've been a soldier, Pedro,' Brogan said to the ex-soldier. 'What do you reckon he'll do?'

'He say as I do,' translated Jose. 'All that is left for him is a direct attack. We do not know how many men with guns he can call on but it is certain to be far more than we have in the village.'

'At this moment, I'd say he has about eight or nine,' said Brogan. 'I counted nine of 'em up at the pass. Maybe he can find a couple more, but I think they were all there. It could be that I killed or at least injured two of 'em, but I don't know for sure. We have to assume that he can call on at least nine. More important than how many men he can raise is when he's goin' to do somethin'.'

'Perhaps that will be very soon, Señor Brogan,' said Maria, pointing towards the river. 'He comes, but he looks to be alone.'

Brogan could see James Brindley approaching the ford, where he stopped, obviously waiting for Brogan to come to him. Brogan duly obliged after sending his four men to vantage points just in case.

'You are a man full of surprises,' said Brindley as Brogan squared up to him on the opposite bank. 'Where the hell did you find that dynamite? My men were supposed to have searched everywhere.'

'From what I saw they were more interested in a couple of *señoritas*,' said Brogan.

'Unfortunately you're probably right at that,' said Brindley. 'It's getting so that you just can't trust anyone these days. OK, McNally, you've made your point, you can outthink, outwit and outshoot my men any time you like and I'll even admit that you come pretty damned close to outthinking me. You can probably outshoot me as well, I'll not deny that, I'm not a gunfighter. I could use a man like you. There's a job for you if you want it, McNally. I'll pay you fifty dollars a month, all found. The going rate for a ranch hand in these parts, even one who can use a gun, is ten dollars a month, all found. You won't even have to eat the same food as the others, you can sleep and eat in the main house.'

'You'll be tellin' me next that the deal includes the services of your wife,' said

Brogan, sarcastically.

'There isn't a Mrs Brindley,' replied Brindley, stiffening slightly. 'She died last year giving birth to my son. Unfortunately he died too.'

'Sorry to hear that,' said Brogan, genuinely sorry for his remark. 'I didn't mean no offence, even to you.'

'None taken,' said Brindley. 'You weren't to know. Think about it, McNally,' he continued. 'These people aren't worth bothering with. They're all born losers, just like most Mexicans. I want them out of here soon and if you help me we can both be very rich men.'

'And how can that be, Mr Brindley?' asked Brogan. 'Look at this land. You know as well as I do that it isn't worth that much. I suppose there could be gold but somehow I don't think so. I'm sure it would have been found a long time ago had there been any. It might support a few cows but that's about all and I'm sure you're not interested in sheep or goats. No, Mr Brindley, there's got to be something more to it.'

'Join me and you'll find out what it is,' said Brindley. 'My men keep asking me the same question but none of them knows the truth of it.'

'You tell me what is so important and I'll tell you if I'll join you or not,' said Brogan. 'I can't say fairer'n that.'

'Sorry, McNally,' said Brindley, giving a knowing laugh. 'Nice try, but no deal. I just thought I'd test you out one more time. I'm a pretty good judge of men and somehow I get the impression that money isn't all that important to you. I'd say that as long as you have enough to pay your way, you are a happy man. If I'm right, then I'm wasting my breath.'

'You're wastin' your breath,' confirmed Brogan.

'I thought so,' said Brindley, giving a broad smile. 'You know, McNally, I even envy you. Life is probably a whole lot easier for not chasing dollars. Money can be a curse as well as a blessing. OK, at least I now know for certain where I stand. I actually like you, McNally, but I shan't have any difficulty in killing you myself. Oh, yes, I can assure you that you and anyone else in this village who stands against me will die and that it will be very soon.'

'Thanks for the warning,' said Brogan. 'Seems to me I been hearin' threats like that all my life. I ain't sure just how old I am but I reckon I'm over fifty years old now. Age ain't important as far as I'm concerned since I ain't got no plans on retirin'. I've heard words like that for all them years and, as you can see, Mr Brindley, I'm still here. OK, so just maybe you'll be the one who proves himself right an' me wrong. That's life though. One of these days, though, I've got to die, we all have.'

'I'm too young to die,' said Brindley with a laugh. He turned his horse and spurred it forward.

Brogan was joined by the others and for a few moments they watched as Brindley disappeared.

'I could have killed him,' said Manolo.

'Yeah, maybe you could,' said Brogan. 'Maybe I'm wrong but killin' like that just don't seem right.'

'*Sí*,' replied Manolo 'I understand what you mean. Father Alonso, he would have agreed with you. It is still a pity, I had him in my sights. All I had to do was squeeze the trigger; it would have been easy.'

'Talkin' of Father Alonso,' said Brogan. 'Are you certain you've searched everywhere. There must be a very good reason Brindley wants this land so much and if anyone knew the answer it would be your priest.'

'I think he know why,' said Maria who had also joined them. 'Many times I talk to him and he says he knows many things about Señor Brindley.'

'What did he actually say?' asked Brogan.

'He actually say nothing,' said Maria. 'He talk about Señor Brindley but he really say nothing at all but I think he know the reason.'

'I know you're a very clever girl,

Maria,' said Brogan, 'but unless he taught you how to talk to the dead you're not saying anythin' useful either.'

'I cannot talk to him but I am sure that somewhere he has written down what he knows,' said Maria.

'I would have thought so too,' said Brogan.

'We will search his house again if you wish,' offered Jose. 'But we have looked everywhere including the floors and the walls. If he had written it down surely he would not have made it so difficult to find?'

'Then all I can say is we've been lookin' in the wrong place,' said Brogan. 'Have you searched the church properly?'

'If we search the house and the church any more they will fall down,' said Jose, 'but I suppose we can try again.'

'I don't suppose it'll do any good,' said Brogan. 'In any case, right now Brindley is a bigger problem than anythin' Father Alonso did or did not know. I don't suppose any of you has a map of this area?'

'A map,' said Jose, giving a broad smile. 'Why would anybody want a map of Los Cahuillas? There is nothing worth showing. Everybody in Los Cahuillas they know this land well, they do not need a map.'

'A map can show where and how somebody might do somethin',' said Brogan. 'I didn't really expect one, it was just an idea. OK, I need to think. I'm pretty sure nothin' is goin' to happen just yet. I'll be back.'

He walked along the river, following it downstream. What he was looking for he really had no idea, all he wanted to do was get some impression of the land surrounding the village.

He walked about half a mile and found himself at the top of a hill. The river, now forty or fifty feet below him, disappeared into thick woodlands and he decided not to go any further.

His view from the hill gave him a different perspective of Los Cahuillas and he saw that it actually stood at the junction of four valleys. Two of them ran more or less north and south and two east and west. The one to the north, the one he was now looking along, was quite wide and well wooded. The other three were given over to mainly grassland.

The valley which led to James Brindley's ranch seemed to be the shortest of the four and he could just about make out the now blocked pass. That apart, there was nothing to be seen. The only thing that was obvious was that if Brindley was to attack he would have to use this short valley or make a very long detour. The fact that it was blocked might make it difficult to drive cattle along, but it could be quite easily negotiated by a man on a horse.

Brogan made his way back to Los Cahuillas without a plan of any sort. Any future actions were totally dependent upon Brindley. All he could do was wait and see what happened. Whilst his four men might well be able to hold

Brindley's men at bay for a short time, it would be nothing more than a delaying tactic: they did not have access to very much ammunition.

'If you got any sense at all, McNally,' he said to himself, 'you'll get the hell out of it right now.'

'Can't quit now though,' he replied to himself. 'Things have only got this far on account of you interferin'. You owe it to 'em to at least try.'

'Teach you to mind your own business though, won't it?'

'Maybe so.' He sighed.

The mood in the village was one of quiet resignation. A few, led by the headman, Miguel, were already heading for the hills but, strangely, the majority seemed to want to stay. Jose and Manolo were once again searching the church and Father Alonso's adobe. This time they were tearing everything apart.

'There is nothing, Señor McNally,' said Jose. 'If we knew what we are looking for it might help but even then we find nothing.'

'I didn't really expect you would,' said Brogan. 'It looks like your head-man, Miguel, was right. You can't fight Brindley. I should never have put you up to it. I'm sorry. I suggest you tell everyone to pull out now, before it's too late. You can't hope to hold out against Brindley.'

'It is already too late,' said Jose. 'Those who wish to leave are doing so. The rest of us remain and we shall die fighting if we have to.'

'A noble sentiment,' said Brogan. 'Futile but noble. I need a drink. Can I help myself to your beer?'

'Be my guest, *señor*,' said Jose. 'Perhaps I shall join you shortly.'

Maria was in the cantina as Brogan entered. She smiled broadly when she saw him.

'You asked about a map, Señor Brogan,' she said. 'I have found just what you ask for.'

'I said you were a very surprising and resourceful girl,' said Brogan. 'It's just a pity you can't find us more guns. Where did you find it?'

'The old man, Señor Callista,' she replied. 'I remembered that there was such a thing in a drawer in his room.' With a rather theatrical flourish she produced a tattered-looking sheet of paper, but it was quite definitely a map. 'How can such a thing help defeat Señor Brindley?' she continued.

'I ain't got the faintest idea,' admitted Brogan. 'All I wanted was to get some idea of the lie of the land.'

He spread the map out on a table and stared down at it for a few moments. Los Cahuillas was clearly marked, as were the four valleys, but there was no indication of Brindley's ranch. He was not very surprised: there was a date at the top of the map which was twelve years old.

However, there were two inked-in lines and they looked as though they had been made far more recently. The ink and colouring of the map was generally faded but these two lines were much darker and, in Brogan's opinion, had not had time to fade.

One of the lines ran down the north-south valleys, and the other along the east-west valleys. They crossed in the centre of Los Cahuillas which was circled. For some time Brogan puzzled over the possible meaning of the lines: it seemed that they probably indicated roads or trails of some kind.

'You're a bright girl,' he said to Maria. 'What do you think? Did your old friend ever say anythin'?'

'I find him looking at the map a few times,' she said. 'But he never say anything to me. Once I find him and Father Alonso looking at it but I do not know what they talk about. The only thing was that Father Alonso, he seem very excited. This was about a year ago, perhaps not even that long. I remember that it was soon after this that Señor Brindley he start to make trouble.'

'That might just be a coincidence,' said Brogan. 'Thing is, I'd say these lines indicate a road, a trail or somethin' like that. It has to be. Why else would anybody draw lines which followed what looks like the lowest ground?'

'*Sí*' agreed Maria, 'but there are roads along those valleys already. They have been there since time began.'

'That's the part that don't make sense,' said Brogan.

'Perhaps you do not ask the right question,' said Maria.

Brogan mumbled to himself and stared at the map for some considerable time. Suddenly he stood up straight and smiled.

'You're right about not askin' the right question,' he said.

'And you now ask the right question?' she urged.

'Has anybody ever talked about the stagecoach comin' this way?' he asked. 'That'd make some sort of sense. Maybe even two stageoaches, using Los Cahuillas as a staging-post.'

'Not as far as I can remember,' she replied. 'Perhaps my uncle he will know something.'

'Better still,' said Brogan, 'we ask your friend.'

Maria laughed lightly. 'I fear you will get little sense from him, Señor Brogan. His mind it is no longer with his body. It wanders all over the place. He is very close to death.'

'Well, we can but try,' insisted Brogan. 'Perhaps if you're there with me it might help. He knows and trusts you.'

'As you say, señor,' she said, 'we can but try.'

Maria led Brogan to the small abode where they found the old man apparently asleep. Brogan actually thought he was dead because he did not appear to be even breathing. He certainly looked like a corpse. Maria, however, was quite certain that the old man was still alive.

At first he did not respond to Maria, but suddenly his eyelids flickered and after a short time his eyes opened and he stared at the ceiling. However, although his eyes were open, they did not seem to see anything.

'It is I, Maria,' said Maria, whispering in his ear. 'Señor McNally, he is with me. He wishes to ask a question. Do you understand?' The old man's eyelids flickered and for a brief moment he looked at Maria. 'He hears us,' Maria said to Brogan. 'Perhaps it will be better if I ask the question in Spanish. He speaks good English but I think his mind it is thinking only in Spanish. It is understandable, especially since he is so close to death.'

'Go ahead,' agreed Brogan. 'Just ask him what the lines he and Father Alonso drew on the map mean.'

Maria nodded and talked to the old man in Spanish. His eyes moved slightly as she was talking but his face remained expressionless. Maria looked at Brogan for a moment and spoke to the old man once again. This time he most definitely looked at her and his lips moved slightly. She moved her ear close to his mouth.

'He says money, much money,' she

said. She moved her ear close to his lips again. 'He says no Brindley.' She spoke gently to the man again but this time there was absolutely no response apart from his eyelids closing.

'Much money and no Brindley,' said Brogan. 'That sounds pretty clear to me but it don't tell us what them lines mean. Ask him again.'

Maria spoke to the old man again but this time there was no response. Eventually she stood up and smiled down at him.

'I think his time it is very soon,' she said.

'Yeah, OK,' said Brogan, rather disappointed. He looked round the small room. 'Is there any chance he might have written somethin' down?' he asked. 'Maybe even Father Alonso left some information here.'

Maria smiled at Brogan. 'I have not been idle, Señor Brogan,' she said. 'Ever since you ask about the map I think is there anything else here? I remembered the map and while I find it I look for something else. I find two letters written to his wife many years ago and I find a piece of paper which says he buys three goats from a nearby village, also many years ago. I find nothing else. However, if you wish I will look again.'

'I don't suppose it'll do any good,' said Brogan. 'The chances are that he would have kept any other information with the map. Still, I suppose you'd better make sure. In the meantime I'll ask your uncle if he knows anythin' about any stagecoaches comin' this way. If he should come round again, remember to ask him what those lines mean.'

Jose had heard nothing about stagecoaches coming through Los Cahuillas and he claimed that nobody else had either. He also maintained that had anyone heard anything at all, it would soon have become common knowledge. Brogan showed him the map.

'I have never seen this before,' he

said. 'The writing of the date at the top, it looks very much like the writing of Father Alonso. I am not very good at writing but I have seen Father Alonso's writing many times. In fact we have the register so we can compare the writing.' He produced the register. 'See, the numbers, the way they are written, they look very much like the writing of the numbers on the map. I think perhaps this map belong to Father Alonso.'

'More'n likely,' agreed Brogan. 'That don't tell us what the hell them lines mean though.'

'I do not believe it could be a stagecoach,' said Jose. 'Why would any stagecoach come this way. From where would they come and to where would they go? The one to the south could only head for the border to Mexico and there is nothing but desert once across the border. There is no large Mexican town.

'Nothing?' queried Brogan. 'Nothing at all?'

'There is nothing as far as I know,' confirmed Jose.

At that moment the ex-soldier, Pedro, came in. He peered over Brogan's shoulder at the map. Jose explained in Spanish what had happened. He apparently asked about the lines as he pointed to them. Pedro thought for a moment before replying.

'He agrees with me,' said Jose. 'There is nothing across the border on the Mexican side except desert. However, he say that there are three *Americano* military forts on this side. They are about fifty miles apart.'

'And forts need supplies,' said Brogan. 'OK, just maybe that explains the line down through the south valley. It could be some sort of supply route. What about the ones goin' east to west?'

'If we knew where the lines they come from and to where they go, perhaps it would make some sense,' said Jose. 'There are many towns to the east but to the west there are only a few.

No, Señor McNally, I can see no logic or sense.'

'Well, makin' sense or not,' said Brogan, 'I got me this feelin' this map's the key to what Brindley's interest is.'

7

During the next twenty-four hours, Brogan was rather surprised by the lack of action from James Brindley. He was not so simple-minded as to think that he had in some way frightened the rancher; he thought it far more likely that Brindley was consolidating and planning his next move. Brogan had detailed his men to take turns at keeping watch, but it seemed to be something of a waste of time.

However, the respite did give Brogan the opportunity to talk to those villagers still remaining. He also sent Jose to track down those villagers who had left and to ask them if they might know anything. He knew that it was a rather forlorn hope but it was just possible somebody had overheard something either the priest or the old man had said.

In his experience there was always at least one who seemed to know every minute detail of everything and everyone in any town or village. In the case of Father Alonso this would probably be the woman who cooked and cleaned for him and such a woman invariably considered herself in some way superior to everyone else in the village.

He did locate the woman who had tended the priest but either she felt that she could not betray anything she might have seen or overheard or — as Brogan felt was really the case — she genuinely knew nothing. In fact of all those villagers he talked to it was plain that no one knew anything. The only one who apparently did know something was the old man and he was obviously in no condition to tell anyone.

Whilst Brogan knew that it was important to know just why Brindley wanted the land so badly, he also knew that in the meantime he had to somehow prevent the villagers being driven out. There was no real reason for this but he felt obliged to help them as best he could.

That was his nature. However, with only four men with guns and a very limited quantity of ammunition he realized that the odds were very much stacked against success. He had the feeling that whatever he did would be largely a waste of time and effort, but nevertheless he felt he had to try.

Maria had agreed to stay with the old man and, should he regain consciousness, ask him what the map meant. This appeared to be another forlorn hope, since every time Brogan checked he found that the old man had not even flickered an eyelid and did not even seem to be breathing. However, Maria assured him that the old man was still alive.

Jose eventually returned with the not unexpected news that there was no news or information. The only thing he had discovered was that the headman, Miguel, had seen at least four men with James Brindley about a year previously, apparently surveying the roads and approaches to the village.

He had not thought much of it at the time, believing that Brindley was probably looking at the land with a view to buying it and running cattle.

The only thing which did not fit in with this idea was that another villager who had been with Miguel at the time, seemed to believe that the men with Brindley were more interested in the roads leading to Los Cahuillas than the surrounding land. He said that they also appeared very interested in the northern forest. It was another small piece of the puzzle but in itself it did not tell Brogan anything.

★ ★ ★

It was about five o'clock in the evening when, for no obvious reason, Brogan suddenly felt a very definite sense of unease. He had such feelings from time to time and over the years he had learned never to ignore them as they invariably turned out to be justified. As a precaution he ordered his four men into position, placed himself near the ford and waited for the expected assault.

About two hours passed and the sun was setting but there was still no sign of Brindley or his men. Brogan was beginning to think that for once his senses had let him down. This thought seemed confirmed when the two boys, Miguel and Pablo, suddenly appeared on the opposite side of the river.

'We have been up to the pass, Señor Brogan,' called Miguel. 'We wanted to see what damage you did to it.'

'That was a damned stupid thing to do,' complained Brogan, more annoyed that the boys had managed to slip away without his knowledge than anything else. 'I'm expectin' Brindley to attack the village at any moment now. You ought to be here where somebody can keep an eye on you.'

'We can look after ourselves, Señor,' said Miguel, proudly. 'There is nobody up there. There is nothing up there except many rocks.'

'Then it looks like I was wrong,' muttered Brogan, now even more annoyed. 'It was still a darned stupid thing to do.'

'If you are expecting him we shall return and wait for Señor Brindley,' said Miguel. 'We will tell you if he comes. Do not concern yourself about us, we can find our way in the dark. We have done so many times.'

Before he could prevent them the boys raced off and were soon lost amongst the rocks and brush. In a way Brogan was thankful to have them acting as look-outs. He knew that the boys were more than capable of looking after themselves and that they would let him know as soon as anything happened. For the moment, though, it appeared that for once his senses had let him down and that he had been a little too cautious.

The sun had disappeared, the sky had darkened and still there was no sign of Brindley. Despite this and the assurance from the boys that Brindley was not in the pass, the feeling that all was not as it might appear persisted and, if anything, over the next half-hour it intensified.

Brogan had always prided himself on his senses and feelings and in the event this occasion proved to be no exception. The only difference was that things did not happen either in the order or from the direction he had expected . . .

★   ★   ★

The first indication that something was about to happen was when Brogan's keen hearing picked up the distant rumble of what might be cattle on the move. However, having earlier looked at the map, he dismissed the idea that Brindley had somehow managed to get a herd across the mountain and behind the village.

The rumbling steadily grew in intensity and there was something about the sound which told Brogan that it was not cattle which were on the move, but horses. His hearing and gut feeling also told him that there were far more horses than Brindley had men.

The sound slowly grew louder and the pace of the animals plainly quickened. Suddenly Brogan found himself running towards the village, calling out to the others. Some had plainly heard the sounds as well and several were gathered at the edge of the village and looking towards the expected direction.

The horses were now obviously very close and there were several distant shots and a few loud calls. Quite suddenly, in the gloom, Brogan could just make out many horses heading for the village.

They were obviously being stampeded. The sight and sound was unmistakable and it seemed too late to do anything about them. Stampeding animals were almost impossible to stop.

At least forty horses eventually came into full view, apparently from the west, the completely opposite direction to any expected attack. In the now poorer light and amongst the dust being raised, it was almost impossible to make out which horses were being ridden and which were not. The only obvious sign was that the riders on some of them also carried flaming torches.

Even before the horses actually appeared some of the villagers fled into the darkness, whilst others sought protection inside their houses. It seemed that those fleeing the village had made the wiser choice.

Flaming torches were hurled through doorways and windows and even on to roofs. Those thrown through windows and doors very quickly set the interiors ablaze and a few more people, mainly women and children, fled into the darkness. There did not appear to be any obvious attempt to kill any of the villagers. The loose horses thundered through the village, forcing Brogan to take shelter.

They did not appear to do any actual

damage and were very soon clear of the buildings, racing through the ford and heading up towards the pass. A very brief glance told Brogan that there were no riders amongst them.

Three of Brogan's four gunmen had foolishly attempted either to stop or to divert the horses and had apparently been injured in the process. The one exception was the ex-soldier, Pedro, who remained where he was. There had been several shots but it was impossible to tell if they were fired by the four villagers or the attackers. However, with three of his men apparently out of action, Brogan guessed it had been Brindley's men who had fired. What they were shooting at he did not know, there were no obvious targets.

By the time the stampeded horses had disappeared across the ford and up towards the pass, at least six adobes were well alight and those villagers who had taken refuge inside those homes which were not on fire were now in turn fleeing into the surrounding land.

There were a number of shots from behind the adobes followed by brief squeals of pigs and the painful bleatings of goats and sheep. It seemed that Brindley and his men were shooting any penned-up livestock.

During this time — which had actually been very short — Brogan had been unable to draw a line on any rider. Briefly, however, the fires had the effect of highlighting the men on horseback and for the first time Brogan was able to get a clear shot at one of them. He saw the man fall but it was obviously not a fatal shot as he was hauled up behind another rider. Everything was moving so quickly that Brogan found it impossible to get in another accurate shot.

Again, quite suddenly and almost as though they had reacted to a signal, the riders turned their horses round the back of the adobes and then on towards the ford. There was nothing Brogan could do to stop them.

Apart from the occasional crackling

of burning wood, a strange silence fell on the village and for a few minutes nobody, including Brogan, made a move. This silence was suddenly broken by the distressed wailing of a woman as she returned to watch her home burn. After a few more minutes, when it became obvious that nothing else was going to happen, the other villagers started to return. They did their best to put out the fires but were fighting a losing battle.

After a short time Jose, who seemed to be limping quite badly, approached Brogan. He gave Brogan a self-conscious grin.

'I try to stop the horses,' he said. 'The horses they do not listen. My leg, I think it is broken.'

'It don't pay to try an' stop bullets or stampedin' horses,' said Brogan. 'Hell, I should've expected somethin' like that.'

'He did not succeed with the cows,' said Jose, 'there was no reason to think that he would try such a thing again.'

'That's just it,' complained Brogan.

'He knew we'd expect him to try somethin' different. Well, I guess in a way he did just that. It sure 'nough caught me out. Was anybody killed?'

'No,' confirmed Jose. 'It would seem the men were under orders not to shoot. Seve Hidalgo says that one of them pointed his gun at him and said that this time he was lucky, they were not going to shoot anyone.'

'What about your animals?' Brogan asked. 'I thought I heard them shooting at them.'

'They are being looked at now,' said Jose. 'It seems that some are dead and that others are injured. Already those too badly injured are being put out of their agony. I do not know how many.'

Pedro, the ex-soldier, suddenly appeared at Brogan's side and pointed towards the river. Jose translated as Pedro spoke.

'He say that Señor Brindley he is asking for you. He is on the other side of the river.'

'I guess I shouldn't be surprised,' said Brogan. 'OK, I'll go see what he has to say. I reckon I know the answer to that though.'

Brogan could just make out the figure of James Brindley on horseback on the opposite bank. He could not tell if any of his men were behind him, but he suspected they were.

'Do I make my point clear, McNally?' said Brindley.

'Got to hand it to you, Brindley,' said Brogan. 'I wasn't expectin' you to try that kind of thing again and certainly not from that direction.'

'Which just goes to show that I can strike whenever and from whatever direction I choose,' said Brindley. 'I hope that nobody was killed. I gave strict orders that there were to be no killings this time. Despite what you might believe, Mr McNally, I am not a killer.'

'But you can't promise that next time there won't be any killings,' said Brogan. 'I think we get the message.'

'I have something to show you and the Mexicans,' said Brindley, laughing loudly. He waved his arm and two riders appeared out of the darkness. Brogan held back a gasp but his heart sank. 'I think you know these two boys,' continued Brindley. 'I have to admit that I admire their guts and spirit, they put up quite a struggle. Such qualities are rare in any Mexican. One of them even bit one of my men quite badly. Unfortunately I think the boy has now lost a few teeth.'

'Let 'em go, Brindley,' snapped Brogan. 'They're only kids, they ain't done no harm to nobody — 'ceptin maybe the man they bit.'

'In the normal way I would do just that,' admitted Brindley, 'But — and I think you will agree with me — these are anything but normal times. At least as far as I am concerned. It is vital to my plans that this village be cleared in two days' time and that everybody is well clear of here. I shall not even attempt to explain, Mr McNally, suffice to say that it will be cleared one way or another. If the villagers have not gone of their own free will by midday tomorrow, I fear I shall have no alternative but to kill these boys. As you say, they are only young boys and as such entirely innocent. However, I have long since learned that even the innocent must suffer on occasion. I hope it will not be necessary but the first will die just after midday tomorrow and the second early the next morning.'

'And if they do leave?' asked Brogan.

'Providing they have left by midday tomorrow and I am satisfied that they are well clear, the boys will be returned unharmed,' assured Brindley. 'However, just in case somebody — namely yourself — has some idea about these peons returning to claim their land, the boys will not be returned until after my business has been concluded. I hope I make myself clear, Mr McNally.'

'Perfectly,' admitted Brogan. 'If the villagers do agree to what you demand, what sort of guarantee do they have that the boys will be set free?'

'Simply my word,' said Brindley,

giving a laugh. 'I am a man of my word, Mr McNally. I shall trust them to keep their word and they must trust me. I suggest that you put my proposal to the village headman.'

'There will be no need for that, Señor Brindley, Miguel has already left.' The voice of Jose came from behind Brogan. 'I have heard what you have to say. I shall inform the others.'

'Ah, yes, Jose the cantina owner,' said Brindley. 'Then I must assume you are more or less in charge now. Mr McNally cannot help you now and even if he does have any ideas about rescuing the boys you would be wise to forget them. He has done all he can for you, although unfortunately he has done little else but make matters worse.'

'I shall put what you say to the others in the village,' said Jose. 'It is not a decision I can take on my own. Even Miguel must gain the approval of the village elders.'

'Then do it,' said Brindley. 'Just remember, you have until midday tomorrow. If you are not on your way by then, the first of the boys will die. Do not make the mistake of thinking I would not do it, Jose. I *will* kill these boys and then I will still drive you off this land. The next time, however, my men will be under orders to kill every man, woman and child still in the village.'

'You can't get away with this, Brindley,' said Brogan. 'This ain't Mexico. Here there are laws against what you are doin'. What happens when these folk tell the authorities?'

Brindley laughed long and loud. Eventually he replied.

'Authorities! What authorities? Who do you think the authorities are, McNally? They will do what I tell them to do. And in any case just whom do you think they will believe?' he asked. 'Even if you were able to tell anyone what happened, do you think they would take the word of a dirty saddlebum and a few dishevelled Mexican peons? I have many influential friends, you and they have none. It has been suggested in the past that these people are here illegally, that they probably came from the other side of the border.'

'That is where you are wrong, Señor Brindley,' said Jose. 'It is well known that this land was part of Mexico long before the gringo arrive. It is unfortunately true that we have no documents which can prove that we own this land but we do have a register which proves when and where we were all born and that was here, in Los Cahuillas. It was kept by the priest, Father Alonso and the priests before him. It also shows that there has been a village here for more than one hundred years and lists all their names.'

'Very interesting, I'm sure,' said Brindley. 'I dare say if you dig a little deeper you will discover that there were Indians here first. They were here long before the Spanish arrived. Some say they were here for thousands of years. The Indians probably have more right to claim this land than you have but I am sure you will agree they have no case. Midday tomorrow, Jose. As for this register of yours, you will hand it over to me. I have just made it another condition for the release of the boys.'

Brindley spoke to his men and suddenly all were lost in the darkness.

'We have no choice,' said Jose, sadly. 'He has won. In our hearts I suppose we always knew he would. Even with your help, we could not hope to beat a man like that'

'You're leaving?' asked Brogan.

'It is all very well for you, Señor McNally,' said Jose, giving a deep sigh. 'Those boys, they are not your sons.'

'Don't you even want to know what is so damned important about this place?' asked Brogan.

'Whatever it is, it is not as important as the lives of Miguel and Pablo. We cannot be responsible for their deaths.'

'No, but — '

'No, Señor McNally, there are no buts,' said Jose. 'We thank you for all that you have tried to do, *Señor*, and it helps to prove that there are some good people in this world, even good gringos. Father Alonso once told us that the life of even one small child is worth far more than all the gold in the world and, as ever he was right. We leave at dawn.'

True to his word, Jose consulted the others and it appeared that the decision to leave was unanimous amongst the villagers. Even at that late hour many set about gathering their world together.

Brogan realized that he would never persuade them to remain and he did not attempt to try. He eventually found himself outside the home of the old man. Maria was still inside and looked at him sadly as he entered.

'You have heard about the boys, Miguel and Pablo?' he asked her. She nodded. 'I blame myself, I should have kept an eye on them,' he continued. 'I should have known they might do somethin' stupid an' get caught.'

'*Sí*, I have heard,' she replied. 'Do not blame yourself, *Señor*. They are wilful boys, they are always in trouble. Unfortunately Uncle Jose is right, we have no choice but to leave.'

'What about him?' asked Brogan, nodding at the old man.

'I do not believe that he will survive even a short journey,' she said. 'He has not opened his eyes since you were here last.' She tenderly wiped the old man's forehead with a damp cloth. 'The fever, it comes back. See, he sweats. Soon he will have no water left in his body with which to sweat any more.'

'So that's it then,' said Brogan. 'Brindley has beaten you.'

'No, Señor Brogan,' she replied, giving him a tearful smile. 'Señor Brindley, he has succeeded in driving us from our village, but he has not beaten us. We shall find another place and we shall continue with our lives as before. We still have sheep and goats, a few pigs and some chickens. We shall not starve. Eventually I shall marry and have children and I shall recount to them how this strange *Americano* tried to save our village. You will become a legend, Señor Brogan.'

'Imagine that,' said Brogan. 'Brogan McNally, a livin' legend.'

'The heroes of legend might be immortal in many ways, *Señor*,' she said, giving him a broad smile, 'but they have one thing in common, they are always dead. It will be many years before I marry and my children are old enough to understand such stories. I do not believe even you will survive that long. Old age will take you even if a bullet does not.'

'Yeah, guess so,' grunted Brogan.

There seemed little else that Brogan could do and he simply wandered about the village for some time. Jose invited him into the cantina for a beer, which he accepted, but it was plain that everyone was far too busy to pay him much attention. He drank a couple of beers, saddled his horse and wandered off into the darkness.

Nobody had told Brogan where the Brindley ranch actually was, but in the event it did not take much finding. The main building was well lit and there seemed to be a certain amount of coming and going. He was about 500 yards away, too far away to be able to see if Miguel and Pablo were amongst those moving about.

He thought it most unlikely that they would be. Brindley was already well aware that the boys had minds of their own. They would be locked away somewhere safe. However, Brogan needed to know just where they were before he made his move. Riding in and causing mayhem — something he knew he could quite easily do — would achieve nothing.

In actual fact, finding somewhere to hide his horse proved something of a problem and for some time Brogan wandered silently and unchallenged amongst the outbuildings.

Outside the ranch compound there did not appear to be any cover at all. Even though it was dark, he could see that there were no trees and no large rocks.

He narrowly avoided being seen on two occasions but he eventually decided to leave his horse in a large barn amongst some others. He could only hope that, should anyone come in, they would not notice that one of the horses was still saddled.

When he had left the village, Brogan had also taken another four sticks of dynamite. If nothing else they would come in very useful for creating a diversion. He took the dynamite and his rifle and slipped out into the night.

8

Immediately opposite the barn there was a single-storey, wooden building which, judging by the rather dim light and the occasional sound of laughter, seemed to be a bunkhouse. Brogan slowly and silently circled the building and confirmed that it was indeed a bunkhouse.

He peered through a grimy window and saw about eight men. Most were lounging on their bunks but three were playing cards. He was quite certain that he would not find the boys there. There did not appear to be anyone else about so he quickly and silently headed across the large open space between the bunkhouse and the main house.

The house was a large, two-storey and rather rambling building. Once again he slowly circled the building. He stopped every now and then to listen and to peer through windows. There was little to be seen and the house seemed to be empty. Only two of the rooms had lamps burning inside and in one of them he saw James Brindley. He appeared to be reading a book. There was certainly nothing else that gave him a clue as to where Miguel and Pablo might be.

At the rear, alongside the main building, there was a smaller, single-storey building. There was a short covered passageway between it and the main house. This building proved to be the kitchen and seemingly the domain of a negro cook and his wife. Brogan assumed the man to be the cook since it was he who was apparently preparing some food. There was still no sign of the boys but Brogan realized that they would probably be fed so, if anyone knew where they were, it would be the cook and his wife.

There were several small outbuildings and a large barn at the rear of the house and it did not take Brogan long to establish that the smaller buildings were all unlocked and were nothing more than storesheds. The barn was plainly just that, a barn in which was stored hay and timber.

He eventually returned to the kitchen where he secreted himself in a dark corner alongside a water-butt and waited for something to happen. If nothing else, Brogan McNally was very good at waiting for things to happen.

Of course, he knew that he could always make things happen, but at that moment he felt that it would achieve nothing. When he had located the boys would be the time to create a diversion should it prove necessary.

Brogan guessed that he had been waiting for about ten or fifteen minutes when there was something of a disturbance. It seemed to come from the direction of the bunkhouse but eventually it died down. About five minutes later James Brindley crossed from the house into the kitchen.

Brogan could not hear what was said

but after a short time Brindley returned to the house and after a few more minutes the woman placed some food on a wooden tray, lit a candle and then she too crossed into the house. Brogan was quick to try and find out, as best he could, where she went, whilst keeping well into the shadows and remaining outside.

He lost sight of the woman for a short time but then, through a window, caught a glimpse of candlelight and saw her, tray still in hand, heading towards a corner of the house which was in darkness. Once again he lost sight of her but when she reappeared she was carrying the empty tray at her side.

A quick dash by Brogan to where he had first seen James Brindley confirmed that he was in that room. Brogan returned to the darkened corner of the house.

He was now certain that he had located the boys. At least he had located them as far as two or three rooms and that was all he needed to know for the moment. His problem now was to gain access without disturbing anyone.

There were two windows on the side of the building and he attempted to peer through both. Even though it was dark inside it was obvious that the first room was empty. The second window had drapes which were drawn across and he could not see inside.

Something told him that he was probably wasting his time but he gently tapped the window. As expected, there was no response. He even risked tapping a little harder just in case the boys might be asleep but still there was no response.

As far as he could tell these were the only two rooms on that corner of the house, they were certainly the only windows but he realized that it was possible there was another room, one without windows which would be more secure. He did try tapping the window again, this time quite hard and loud but there was still no response.

However, simply on the basis that the

woman had taken food to somewhere in that corner of the house, he was certain that this was where the boys were being kept, but now he was also quite certain the two rooms with the windows were not the only rooms.

It seemed that he had little alternative but to get inside the house and the easiest and most obvious way to do that was through the back door by the kitchen. With apparently only the two negro servants and James Brindley himself to worry about, somewhat arrogantly he did not envisage any problems.

The cook and his wife were now lounging in a couple of chairs and they were both obviously enjoying one of the perks of their position. The man had a bottle of whiskey alongside him and the woman a bottle of gin. Brogan steeled himself and slid past silently. Had they looked up they would have been bound to see him, but they did not.

Once inside there were only two ways to go. One followed a long passage and plainly led to the far rooms, the other, a much shorter passage, led towards the darkened corner. Mr James Brindley was obviously a man of wealth and taste. Carpets ran the length of each passage, making it much easier for Brogan to move silently.

Although it was quite dark, there was enough light to see by. There were four doors at the end of the passage which were reached with ease.

The first door opened easily, which in itself told Brogan that the room was empty. He knew that Brindley would not be so stupid as to leave his prisoners in a room with an unlocked door but he did look inside just to make certain. He quietly closed the door again.

The second door was locked but the very short distance between it and the doors on either side appeared to indicate it was little more than a storage cupboard. The only thing which did not quite fit in with this was the fact that he found it strange for

184

such a cupboard to be locked.

The third door also opened into an empty room, which left only a door opposite the other three. He fully expected to find this door firmly locked but, strangely and most unexpectedly, this too opened up to reveal an empty room. It looked as though he had got things wrong.

Brogan looked at the only locked door and decided that he had not got anything wrong and, narrow as the room beyond obviously was, it was the only place the boys could be. However, even in the dim light he could see that getting inside was plainly not going to be that easy.

The door itself was very stout and thick and, more important, obviously opened outwards, into the passage. This fact alone was most certainly not going to help in breaking the door down should it come to that. The stoutness, thickness and outward opening of the door meant that it would take either a very strong man, a very large jemmy or a battering ram to to open it.

Tough as Brogan McNally was, he certainly did not have the muscle power for such a task and, even if he could do it, he knew that he could never hope to break it down in time to rescue the boys and get them clear. The noise he was bound to make would certainly be heard all over the house and probably as far as the outbuildings.

He had heard of locks being shot off doors but he himself had never actually done or even witnessed such a thing. Normally there would be no need either, most doors and locks were rather flimsy things and gave readily under a firm shoulder. It also seemed to him that even should he attempt to shoot the lock, it would achieve nothing simply because it was plainly a very strong mortise-lock.

A quick look at the locks on the other doors showed that they were obviously very expensively made and set into the thickness of the door. He doubted very much if shooting at them would make much difference at all.

He needed the key and it appeared that the key was with the negro woman, who was probably James Brindley's housekeeper, since this was the only door without a key. He somehow had to get that key. In a very vain hope, he tried the keys from the other three doors which, although fitting, would not turn.

Before making his way back to the kitchen, and as a simple precaution, he tapped on the door and listened. At first there was no sound but as he tapped again, this time a little harder, a young voice spoke in Spanish. That was enough, the boys were in that cupboard. He did not reply, not wanting the boys to raise any alarm and he quietly headed for the kitchen.

Once more he secreted himself behind the large water-butt from where he could see everything in the kitchen. The man seemed to be asleep but the woman was now busying herself repairing some clothing. He waited a few minutes hoping that something would happen which might enable him to get inside the kitchen and remove the key.

'You're just wastin' time an' wishin' for somethin' what just ain't goin' to happen,' he said to himself. 'Things like that only happen in kids' stories. If you want that key, Brogan McNally, it looks like you're just goin' to have to make things happen an' go an' get it.'

During all this time he had been carrying his rifle and now, with it in one hand and his Colt in his other, he crept slowly towards the door to the kitchen. He paused for a few moments while he listened. What he was listening for he did not know; it was something he did purely out of habit but it was a habit which had paid dividends on many occasions.

There was nothing to be heard but even so Brogan felt a slight sense of unease. He waited a little longer. Eventually he was satisfied and suddenly burst into the kitchen.

'Just sit right there, don't move an'

don't say nothin',' he ordered. 'I don't want to kill either of you but I assure you that I will if necessary.'

The man, very surprisingly, simply smiled broadly and took another drink of his whiskey. The woman too gave him a broad, toothy smile as she casually put down her sewing. Without saying a word she reached into her apron pocket and took out a key, holding it almost triumphantly.

'I reckon you must be this McNally feller they was all talkin' about,' said the man.

'Yeah,' agreed the woman, 'I reckon you come for them two boys just like they said you would. Nice boys, just like my own two used to be.'

Quite suddenly, Brogan's senses were screaming at him but he knew that it was now too late to prevent the inevitable.

'Shit!' he oathed. 'It looks like I was expected. Good evenin', Mr Brindley.' He turned his head slightly without actually turning round.

'You could say you were expected, Mr McNally,' a voice said sneeringly behind him. 'You obviously heard me behind you. I didn't think we'd made that much noise but plainly we had.'

'I could smell you,' said Brogan. 'I have this ability to know when there's somethin' like a rattler about. I always know which rock to look under.' He still did not turn round and kept his guns pointed at the two servants. 'You an' rattlers have the same smell,' he continued. 'Somethin' like shit.'

'I know exactly what you mean,' said Brindley. 'I could smell you around as well. Mind you, that wouldn't be difficult. Like all saddle tramps I do believe you are allergic to soap and hot water.'

'I ain't sure what that means, but soap just ain't natural,' grunted Brogan.

'It's obvious you don't think so,' said Brindley. 'Still, I don't think you have come here to discuss your ablution arrangements with me. Welcome to my humble house. It is just a pity you haven't come to offer your services.'

'I won't insult your intelligence by sayin' I have,' said Brogan. 'I think you know why I'm here.'

'I do, and it would appear that you have located the two boys,' said Brindley. 'I must congratulate you on getting this far. By the way, I would put those guns down if I were you. You might be a very good gunman but I think that even I might just be able to kill you before you could do any damage to anyone else. In any case there are three of us so one of us is bound to hit you.'

'How'd you know I was here, or was it just a lucky guess? I don't normally give myself away so easy.'

'Your guns, Mr McNally,' repeated Brindley. 'Your guns and that knife I see in your belt.'

If nothing else, Brogan had learned over many years when to fight and when to admit defeat. This was most definitely not the time to fight. He slowly placed both guns and the knife on the table.

'I must be gettin' old,' he muttered.

'Indeed, we are all getting older, McNally,' said Brindley. 'Now, very slowly, step back from the table. I don't want you within arm's reach of those guns. See, I believe in your ability so I'm not taking any chances.'

Brogan did as instructed, breathing a sigh of relief. Another thing he had learned over the years was that if a man was going to be killed, it normally happened within the first few seconds. A man might be allowed to live for a while if he had information but he knew that Brindley did not want information. It was obvious that killing him did not fit in with Brindley's plans.

'So how'd you know I was here?' Brogan asked again.

'Quite apart from the fact that it was something I expected you to try and do, that being your nature I believe,' said Brindley, 'your horse was discovered still saddled. It certainly didn't belong to me or my men and it is such a moth-eaten old nag that we knew it must be yours.'

'I wouldn't let her hear you sayin' things like that about her,' said Brogan. 'She gets very upset about things like that.'

'If you say so, McNally,' said Brindley. 'I prefer talking to people but I can understand a man talking to his horse when he has nobody else. Now you may turn round.' Brogan did as instructed and found himself facing Brindley and two other men, all with guns aimed at him. 'As you can see, it would have been a very simple matter to shoot you, but whether you believe me or not, I am not a killer, I am a businessman.'

'That's not what I've heard,' said Brogan. 'So what are you goin' to do with me?'

'In three days, four at the outside, my business will be concluded,' said Brindley. 'I shall then be the legal owner of all the land surrounding and including the village of Los Cahuillas. For the moment it would not be convenient if I were to kill anyone, which is why I took care not to kill any of the villagers. When my business is completed you will be free to go where you please. The villagers will have found somewhere else to settle and we shall all be happy.'

'They sure didn't seem too happy about havin' to move on,' said Brogan. 'If you wanted that land so bad why didn't you just ride in an' slaughter them all. It's been done before.'

'My dear McNally,' said Brindley. 'That would be far too barbaric. I agree, it would have been quite easy but in actual fact it would have raised far too many questions. This way I can legally claim that the villagers deserted their homes, which laid the entire village open to purchase.'

'They could still claim they were driven out,' said Brogan.

'Perhaps they could,' agreed Brindley. 'However, I am sure you know something of the speed with which the law operates and you will agree that it is painfully slow. Besides, they would need money to pay for a lawyer and they do not have that much money. No, Mr McNally, they will do what all Mexicans do, just shrug their shoulders and get on with their lives.'

'Talkin' about lives,' said Brogan, 'what about Padre Alonso? I hear you murdered him.'

'No, I did not,' said Brindley. 'He was shot by one of my men who thought he was about to shoot me. If you meet the villagers again, Mr McNally, I suggest you ask them if it was usual for Padre Alonso to wear a gun. There were several witnesses amongst them who will probably confirm what happened.'

'I searched the village, Padre Alonso didn't have no gun.'

'Because my men took it,' said Brindley.

'OK, I'll go along with that,' agreed Brogan. 'Maybe now you'll answer me one question. What is so hell-fire important about Los Cahuillas?'

'Questions, questions, always asking questions, McNally,' said Brindley giving a sigh. 'Perhaps you should have been a lawyer and not a saddle tramp.'

'At least bein' my kind of saddle tramp is an honest occupation,' said Brogan. 'That's more than can be said of most lawyers I've met.'

Brindley laughed. 'In that I am in total agreement with you for once,' he said. 'My lawyer is only interested in the money I pay him. Still, that's enough for now, Mr McNally. All your questions will be answered in the fullness of time. For the moment you can join your two young friends in the cupboard. As you have probably worked out, it is a very strong and secure little room. You have probably noticed that the door cannot be very easily forced. I believe it will be strong enough to withstand even your ingenuity.'

Brindley stood aside and indicated that Brogan should head back into the house. The two men stood one each side of the covered passageway, guns aimed at Brogan, making it impossible for him to even contemplate a surprise. The woman laughed, picked up the key and a candle and followed them.

'OK, so you won't tell me what's goin' on,' said Brogan as they walked along the passage. 'You can tell me if you really would have killed the boys though. I have the feelin' it was all bluff, 'specially since you claim you ain't no killer. Strangely enough I believe you. I reckon I'm a fairly good judge of a man.'

'I thank you for that,' said Brindley. 'However, that is something you will never really be certain of. It was, I admit, a threat made more to influence the villagers than you. Unlike you, they will never be sure. All I can say is that I am not a murderer, Mr McNally.'

The woman unlocked the door and for a brief moment the light of the candle lit up the inside of the cupboard. It appeared to be about five feet wide by about six or seven feet deep, which was reasonably large as far as cupboards went. The actual floor space was less than this due to shelving around the walls. The shelves were empty. The boys were sitting hunched on the floor and blinked in the unaccustomed light, avoiding the direct glare.

'I told you your friend Señor McNally would come, didn't I?' said Brindley. 'As you see, I am a man of my word.' Brogan was pushed inside. 'I have no doubt that you will try your best to escape, McNally,' Brindley continued. 'I believe that even you will find it impossible but should you have any ideas and just on the off chance, one of my men will be sitting outside all the time.' He laughed as the woman went to close the door. 'You will find a large bucket in there,' he said. 'You can guess what it's for. It means that there is one less reason for anyone to open this door until they have to. I can't do anything about the smell I'm afraid.'

The woman also laughed and slammed the door and locked it. For a few moments Brogan remained where he was waiting for his eyes to adjust to the darkness. However, the room was so tightly sealed that the only light able to penetrate came from the glow of a candle through the slight gap at the bottom of the door. After a short time even this disappeared and the darkness was indeed total. Eventually Brogan sank to the floor.

'I say to Pablo that you would come, Señor Brogan,' said the voice of Miguel after a time. 'I always knew you would try to rescue us. Unfortunately, *señor*, it would seem that your plan has failed.'

'Who said anythin' about me havin' a plan?' muttered Brogan 'I don't hardly ever make plans.'

'Perhaps it is as well,' said Miguel with a simplicity which annoyed Brogan, but he managed to control his true feelings.

'An' if you ain't got nothin' better to say than things like that, I suggest you keep your mouth shut,' Brogan muttered again.

Realizing that the darkness was total and that his eyes would not adjust any more he resigned himself to the darkness. He contemplated the possibility of breaking the door down but very quickly dismissed the idea. He also felt the walls and decided that somehow breaking through was also completely impractical. The floor was solid stone. It seemed that James Brindley had known exactly what he was doing when he chose this tiny room to house his prisoners.

How long they had been locked away, Brogan simply did not know. Complete darkness somehow had the ability to turn time into a meaningless concept. Quite suddenly, however, a key turned in the lock and Brogan stood up as the door was opened. He blinked in the glare of the light from a candle but was able to make out a guard who had a gun aimed at him. There were two people and the second one turned out to be the woman.

'I brung you some vittles,' she announced. 'It ain't nothin' much, just some bread an' some cheese an' some water. Best make it last, 'specially the water, it's all you is goin' to get until breakfast.' A tray was slid along the floor and the woman laughed. 'Sweet dreams to you all an' don't you go doin' nothin' to them boys your mother or their mothers wouldn't approve of, Mr McNally.'

'As far as I remember my ma never approved of nothin',' said Brogan. 'My tastes certainly don't extend as far as boys if that's what you mean.'

'Glad to hear it,' replied the woman. 'You never can tell these days. I wouldn't trust any one of them hired hands in the bunkhouse with small boys like these two. I hear tell there's some mighty strange folk about. I even heard tell about some of 'em doin' things with animals. Can you imagine that?'

She laughed loudly and the door was once again slammed shut. Brogan pushed the tray into the centre of the floor. 'You heard what she said,' he said to the boys. 'I ain't hungry but don't go drinkin' all the water.'

'We had some food not long ago,' said Miguel. 'We too are not hungry. They feed us very well.' Pablo spoke in Spanish and Miguel translated. 'He

201

asks when you are going to set us free?'

'Just as soon as I can get this door open,' muttered Brogan. 'Now shut up the both of you an' let me do some thinkin'.'

9

The first and only indication that it was morning came when Brogan heard the key turning in the lock. He stood up as the door opened to an almost blinding light through which eventually emerged the laughing features of the house-keeper. She carried a tray which she placed on a shelf.

Brogan noticed there were spoons but no knives or forks on the tray. There being no forks was not at all unusual, very few ranch hands used anything other than a knife and spoon.

Behind the housekeeper stood an armed guard, rifle at his hip but aimed into the doorway. This made any idea of rushing past her a non-starter.

It had been a long night, as least as far as Brogan was concerned. It had been made longer simply by the fact that there had been no way of telling the time. He did have a pocket-watch but in the pitch-dark it had been impossible to see the dial and now he discovered that he had forgotten to wind it up. He had also spent most of the night racking his brain trying to work out how to escape. Unfortunately he had not come up with even a most unlikely solution.

'Here's your breakfast,' the woman announced. 'My man Nathaniel, he looks to have done you proud. You got ham an' eggs an' some real coffee. Now you is honoured with real coffee. I reckon that must've been Mr Brindley's idea. Real coffee is usually only for him.'

'Give my thanks to Nathaniel and Mr Brindley,' muttered Brogan. 'What time is it? Bein' in the dark all night means I lost all sense of time. It could be mornin' or even still night as far as I'm concerned.'

'Nearest I can tell you is it's about half an hour after sunrise,' she replied. 'I ain't never learned to read, write or tell the time. Us old slaves was never taught how to read an' write. It warn't the thing for black folk to be able to do just in case it gave 'em ideas above their station in life. Now you eat your food an' I'll be back. There'll be another man with me an' he'll escort one of you boys to empty that there bucket into the cesspit. I expect you'll be pleased to be rid of it. I smelled me worse but it can't be nice havin' that stink all night.'

'Are you goin' to lock the door?' asked Brogan.

'Them's my orders,' she said. 'Mr Brindley, he was quite specific. Helen, he says to me — Helen, that's my name you see — Helen, he says to me, under no circumstances whatsoever must that saddlebum McNally be allowed out of that room. An' he say I wasn't to take no sweet-talkin' from you to leave the door unlocked. If ever you leave that door unlocked an' he gets out, he says, I'll skin you alive. He sure would too, skin me alive.'

'Well at least can't you let us have

some light? I like to see what I'm eatin'. It tastes better that way.'

Helen thought for a moment and then smiled. 'Mr Brindley didn't say nothin' about you not havin' some light,' she said. 'I don't see why not. I knows it gets pitch-black in there. I knows just how dark it gets on account of the door closed on me once when I was inside. It was so dark I didn't even know which way I was facin'. OK, I tell you what. I'll be back in a couple of minutes an' I'll bring you a candle. Can't do no more'n that. I sure ain't goin' to bring you no oil-lamp though, I ain't that stupid. You could use the oil to start a fire.'

'You seem to have thought of everythin',' said Brogan.

'Just 'cos I ain't got no readin' or writin' don't mean I don't know a thing or two,' she said with a laugh. 'Anyhow, I don't reckon there's enough heat in a candle-flame to start no proper fire. Them walls is made of mud brick an' there sure ain't nothin' in there that'll burn so easy 'ceptin' maybe them shelves, but I don't reckon no candle will set them alight. That door is far too thick for a candle-flame to do any damage to at all. Anyhow, even if you did start a fire I reckon you'd choke to death in the smoke 'fore you got burned to death. Ain't nobody would bother about savin' you, that's for sure.'

'I suppose that just about covers everythin',' said Brogan. 'OK, Helen, I'll settle for just a candle to give us a bit of light.'

Helen laughed and closed the door, taking care to lock it. True to her word, she returned about two minutes later with a lighted candle.

'I decided on just a small candle,' she said, placing it on a shelf. 'I'll be along to see how you is gettin' on later on. If you is lucky I might give you another small candle then.'

'I suppose it might give us an hour of light,' said Brogan, looking hard at the candle.

'An hour is better'n nothin',' she

replied. 'Now eat your breakfast 'fore it gets too cold.' She laughed and closed the door.

The boys seemed fairly hungry and Miguel had to admit that ham and eggs was something of a luxury. Apparently breakfast for them — if they had any at all — normally consisted of a corn or maize porridge or pancakes. Brogan too, although he had not really felt hungry, discovered just how hungry he was. The thing he appreciated the most was the coffee. He was able to have most of it because the boys apparently did not like the taste of real coffee. Fortunately for them there was still some water left from the previous night.

When they had eaten Brogan was able to study his prison in some detail for the first time. Helen had been quite right, the walls were all made of thick, mud brick. The shelving itself, although made of wood, did not, at first glance, offer any means of escape. However, after a short time the germ of an idea started to form in his mind.

The boys looked at Brogan curiously as he started to pull at the strips of shelving fastened to the wall. The actual shelves were not fastened down and he removed some of them. This revealed a framework of battens, which was apparently nailed or screwed to the wall.

After a time he grunted to himself, took one of the spoons and started to force the handle between the wall and the wooden battens. Slowly but surely he was able to remove a strip of batten about four feet long. It had three long nails protruding through it.

'A club, Señor Brogan?' said Miguel, helpfully. 'I think that if you intend to hit anyone with that it will hardly make an impression on them. It is not heavy enough and will break too easily.'

'Smart ass!' muttered Brogan. 'Don't you think I knows that? I ain't about to hit nobody over the head with it. I might just tan the ass of a couple of know-all Mexican kids if they don't keep their mouths shut though.'

Miguel laughed as Pablo said something in Spanish. '*Sí*, I think Pablo is right.' said Miguel. 'He thinks that you make a spear. There is only one problem with that, Señor Brogan, a spear must have a sharp point. We too have made spears but we needed a knife to sharpen them. I do not think a spoon is a good tool with which to make a very sharp point.'

'I could always use your tongue,' Brogan muttered again. 'No, you is right, it does need a sharp point an' again, you is right, we ain't got nothin' to sharpen it with. Since you two is so darned clever, you got any bright ideas?'

Miguel spoke to Pablo and for a short time they talked to each other in Spanish. Eventually Pablo stood up and pointed to one of the long nails which had fastened the baton to the wall.

'Pablo he say you should use a long nail,' said Miguel.

Brogan studied the batten and the three nails protruding through it for a short time. Eventually he slowly forced one of the nails back through the batten.

'Yeah, OK,' he grunted. 'I'd've thought of it eventually.' He then forced the two remaining nails from the baton. 'Only problem is fixin' it to the end.'

'You need some twine, señor,' said Miguel.

'*You need some twine, señor,*' mimicked Brogan. He looked around the shelves. 'Hell, wouldn't you just know it, it looks like we is clean out of twine. Maybe I'll get Helen to bring some.'

'Oh no, Señor Brogan,' said Miguel, triumphantly. 'That will not be necessary. Both me and Pablo, we have twine.' He pulled at the waistband of his baggy trousers. 'How else can we hold up our pants if we do not have string or twine?'

'Miguel,' said Brogan, with a laugh, 'there are times when you do talk sense. What are we waitin' for? I'm sure one of you won't mind losin' your pants.'

The boys looked at each other and giggled. Pablo removed his pants and handed them to Brogan. Brogan soon removed the cord.

The cord was plainly far too thick but Brogan rapidly stripped several strands from it. About ten minutes later he gazed almost lovingly at his handiwork. Pablo threaded the remaining cord back through his trousers and restored his modesty to some extent. Brogan then spent a few minutes sharpening the point of the nail on the stone floor. Eventually he was satisfied.

'I don't know if this is goin' to work,' he said. 'It's the only chance we've got though. Let's hope somebody ain't too long comin' an' let's hope there's only one man with Helen.'

As a precaution, Brogan inserted the two remaining nails back into their holes and eventually succeeded in balancing the flat shelves on them and the front battens. He was satisfied that it would stand up to a brief inspection. All he could do now was wait.

The candle was just beginning to flicker as it reached the end of the wick when the key turned in the lock. Brogan stood back as the door opened, the makeshift spear behind his back. The door opened to reveal Helen, holding another candle, a guard with a gun and, very annoyingly, James Brindley. Brogan did not attempt to use the spear.

'Good morning, Mr McNally,' greeted Brindley. 'I trust you slept well. I thought that I'd tell you that the village is now deserted.'

'We can go then?' said Brogan.

'Oh, no, I'm afraid not, Mr McNally,' said Brindley. 'Three days before my business is completed, I said. I'm afraid you must remain here until it is. I don't want somebody like you roaming the countryside until things are complete. You could make life a little more difficult than it need be. It would seem that the villagers ignored my instruction to hand over that register, but it doesn't really matter. It's not as if it was anything like deeds to the land, is it?'

'I guess not,' agreed Brogan. 'Ain't no need to hang on to the boys though. They can't hurt you none if they go.'

'I agree,' said Brindley. 'However, I am by my nature a very cautious man. I like to have a little in reserve. Insurance I call it. As long as I have the boys I know there will be no trouble from the Mexicans.'

'OK,' said Brogan, 'I guess I can put up with their company and stink for a few days more. Speakin' of stink, didn't you say somethin' about emptyin' this bucket, Helen?'

'I sure did,' said Helen. 'Just as soon as Mr Brindley is on about his business I'll see to it.'

'There will, of course, be an armed guard here at all times,' reminded Brindley. 'I still don't trust you, McNally.'

'I'm flattered,' said Brogan. 'If it means anythin', I don't trust you either. How do I know you won't kill us?'

'You are still alive, are you not,

McNally?' replied Brindley. 'It would have been very easy to kill you before now had I chosen to.'

Brogan had to admit the logic of that statement.

Brindley laughed and marched off down the corridor. For a very brief moment Brogan was tempted to use his new weapon, but he resisted simply because Brindley was too close.

Helen laughed and closed the door and announced that she would return in a few minutes with another candle and to see that the bucket was emptied. It was, in fact, a good ten minutes before she returned by which time the candle had gone out. Brogan did not mind, the lack of light might well make it easier for him to do what he had to do.

Helen opened the door but the guard was not to be seen. He was in fact out of sight leaning against a wall. Helen placed the candle on the makeshift shelf and for a very brief moment Brogan thought it was going to collapse.

'Mr Brindley has gone out for the day,' she said. 'All the hands have gone too, all 'ceptin' Marvin here. He's got a bad back an' can't ride too well. He's been given the job of lookin' after you.'

'Welcome, Marvin,' greeted Brogan.

A thin, smallish man appeared, his pistol aimed at Brogan. 'I might've hurt my back but it ain't affected my shootin' hand,' he said. 'Mr Brindley said to kill you if you should try any funny stuff.'

'Have you ever killed a man before, Marvin?' asked Brogan.

'Sure have,' said Marvin, with a broad grin. 'I shot me two, stabbed one in the heart an' slit the throat of another an' I shattered a man's head with the butt of my rifle. There ain't no need to go through all that guff about how hard it is for a man to kill another man. I was sent to prison for shootin' a man when I was only fourteen. That was my first.'

'A man of great experience,' said Brogan. 'We should get along just fine. I lost count of the number of men I killed.'

'I ain't never yet met no saddlebum what killed a man in an honest fight,' said Marvin, sneeringly. 'I don't reckon you is no different.'

'An' you is both talkin' a load of rubbish,' interrupted Helen. 'Men! You is all the same. If anybody ever believed even half of what you said there'd be hardly any other men left in the world. There ain't one of you knows how to stand up to no woman though, you ain't none of you got the guts for somethin' like that. Now, one of you two boys pick up that bucket an' bring it out here. Just the one of you. Mr McNally, you stays here. Them's Mr Brindley's orders.'

Miguel and Pablo both hesitated, looked at each other and then at Brogan as if they were waiting for him to decide. Helen sighed heavily, made some comment about men and boys being unable to make even simple decisions and ordered Miguel to pick up the bucket.

'Best do as she says,' said Brogan. 'You heard what she said about men havin' no guts.'

Somewhat reluctantly Miguel picked up the bucket and made for the door. It appeared that the bucket was heavier than expected.

'An' don't you dare spill none of that on my clean floors,' said Helen. 'If you so much as spills a single drop I'll make you get down on your hands an' knees an' lick the floor clean.'

Miguel smiled weakly and struggled through the door. Helen stood aside as Miguel turned into the passage and, whilst all attention appeared to be on the boy, Brogan slipped his makeshift spear into a throwing position.

However, before Brogan could do anything, Miguel suddenly cried out and apparently slipped. The bucket crashed to the floor and its contents spilled out, the bulk of it going over Marvin's boots.

'You clumsy young bastard!' yelled Marvin. 'I'll have your guts — '

Marvin never did say exactly what he was going to do with Miguel's guts. Brogan's arm swung the spear with all the force he could muster and an instant later Marvin was staring, obviously unseeingly, the spear protruding from his forehead. There was only the merest hint of blood.

In almost the same instant Brogan was also out in the passage and retrieving Marvin's pistol and rifle. Helen actually seemed rather more concerned about the mess on the floor than the fate of Marvin.

'Sorry about the mess,' said Brogan, almost apologetically but not quite. 'I'm sure Mr Brindley will understand and not blame you for it.'

Helen slowly turned her head and stared at Brogan for a moment. Suddenly a broad smile spread across her face.

'Well, you won me my wager,' she said. 'I told my Nathaniel that you'd figure a way out. He was quite certain you wouldn't stand a chance. We had a five-dollar wager on it. We all knows Marvin here was just about the meanest man there ever was an' that he'd killed a few times. In fact it was Marvin who told Nathaniel that he hoped you would try somethin' just so's he could kill you.'

'Apart from winning five dollars, you seem pleased,' said Brogan.

'I'm glad you is goin' to get them boys out of here,' said Helen. 'It warn't right of Mr Brindley to use them like that. I knows he was thinkin' of handin' them over to the hands so's they could have some fun with them. Now that just ain't right or natural, not men havin' their way with boys. I heard me some strange tales about what they gets up to in that bunkhouse though. I don't know what he was goin' to do with you, he never said nothin'. Now I suggest you gets the hell out of it while you can. Your own guns are in the kitchen an' I think your horse is still in the stable. I ain't sure if she's saddled or not.'

'If you felt like that, why didn't you

help us before?' asked Brogan. 'You had the key.'

'On account of I'm very attached to my skin,' she replied. 'He said he'd skin me alive an' skinnin' alive is just what he'd do. I used to belong to his pa an' when he was a boy, he watched while another slave was skinned alive. He was no more'n the age these boys are now but he seemed to enjoy it. Now will you quit jawin' an' get the hell out of here.'

'I think, for your own safety, that I had better lock you in the cupboard,' said Brogan. 'Nathaniel too, I guess. Marvin's body can be dragged into one of the other rooms, he ain't goin' nowhere.'

'Then do it!' ordered Helen. 'Nathaniel should be preparin' food in the kitchen. Don't you worry none about him, he's terrified of guns an' he's pretty deaf too. We ain't expectin' Mr Brindley back until this afternoon. I hear tell they've gone over to the eastern range so you should have plenty of time to get away.'

Purely as a precaution, Brogan locked Helen in the cupboard before going to fetch Nathaniel. The cook also proved remarkably compliant and in a short time both he and Helen were locked in the cupboard.

Before finally closing the door, Brogan asked them if they had any idea just why James Brindley wanted the land around the village of Los Cahuillas.

'Somethin' about two railroad companies comin' through,' said Helen. 'He wants that land so's he can sell some of it on to the railroad an' then either develop or sell what's left.'

'Two railroad companies?' queried Brogan.

'Yes, sir,' she said. 'One's runnin' east to west an' the other north to south. Where they cross is right in Los Cahuillas. He reckons there'll be a sizeable town there too, an' rich pickin's for whoever owns the land.'

'And he's meeting somebody to buy the land?'

'He already put in his claim but he was told that the villagers had first claim,' she said. 'He could only take it over if the village was abandoned. Now he don't know I knows all this but even if I can't read or write, I got me a good pair of ears. Somebody from the state capital is in cahoots with Mr Brindley. The idea is for Mr Brindley to put up the money an' for this other person to see that the sale goes through smoothly, then they split the profits.'

'Have you any idea who this other person is?'

'No, sir,' said Helen. 'I ain't never seen him either. I think somebody from one of the railroad companies is in on it too.'

'Now you knows as much as we do,' said Nathaniel, speaking for the first time. 'Helen should never have said all them things. Even if nothin' happens, if ever Mr Brindley finds out we told you, we is both dead meat.'

'I can assure you that he'll hear nothing from me,' said Brogan. 'I shall probably confront him with it, but I won't tell him who told me. I'll say I worked it out for myself. He'll probably believe that.'

'Yeah, I reckon he just might,' agreed Helen. 'I heard him say you was just about the brightest man he ever met an' you is wastin' yourself bein' what you are, a saddlebum.'

'My life is mine to waste how the hell I like,' said Brogan. 'What about the men from the railroad companies?'

'They should turn up in two or three days,' said Nathaniel. 'First should be the man from the state capital to sort out ownership of the land an' then the men from the railroad companies.'

'As far as I know,' said Helen, 'apart from one man — I don't know which one or which company — the railroad companies don't know a thing about what's goin' on. Mr Brindley's already told 'em that he owns that land.'

'That explains everythin',' said Brogan. 'Just one more thing. Why the hell are you tellin' me all this?'

Helen laughed. 'We was both slaves once,' she said. 'Still are, I suppose, but what else can we do? Mr Brindley an' his kind think Mexicans an' blacks is lower'n dirt. They don't mind drivin' nobody off their land just so long as they get's paid for doin' it. We knows what it's like to have nothin'. It's too late for us, but not for the likes of Miguel or Pablo here. Now get your ass outa here, Mr McNally.'

Brogan had heard all he needed to hear. He decided to take her advice and get his ass out of it. He locked the door but left the key in the lock, not too worried about them escaping.

Finding his horse also proved very easy. She was one of only three animals in the stable and she appeared to be more interested in her fodder than in Brogan. In fact she seemed quite disgusted when Brogan threw his saddle across her back.

'Sorry about this, old girl,' he apologized. 'You had yourself a good rest, now it's time to do somethin' to earn it. We gotta get out of here fast.'

There was another saddle in the stable which he threw across the back of one of the other horses. When both horses were saddled, Brogan ordered Miguel and Pablo up on to the second horse.

'I had the good idea, no, Señor Brogan?' said Miguel.

'Good idea?' queried Brogan.

'*Sí*, I spill the bucket. It was a good idea, no? I thought it was a good idea and Pablo, he too thought it was a good idea.'

'*Sí*, it was a good idea,' said Brogan. 'You mean to say you did that deliberately? I thought you'd just dropped it because it was too heavy. That's sure what it looked like to me.'

'Oh, no, señor,' said Miguel. 'I did not drop it. It was not very heavy. I have carried much heavier things than that. I just thought it would be a good idea. The idea it came to me as soon as I pick up the bucket. Miguel, I say to myself, I wonder what Señor Brogan he would do if — '

'OK, OK,' grated Brogan. 'It was a wonderful idea, a bloody marvellous idea. I don't know what I would have done without you. Now shut up an' ride.'

10

Much to his surprise, there were four other people in Los Cahuillas when they arrived. The first to greet them was Maria and her excuse for still being there was the old man. She claimed, probably correctly so, that any attempt to move him would be certain to kill him.

There were also two older women, who proved to be the mothers of Miguel and Pablo. They appeared from an adobe, crying and wailing in the manner of most older Mexican women. It seemed to be a way of life rather than real feeling. After an initial emotional reunion, both boys were roundly berated, slapped hard and led away from the village. The horse was left with Brogan. The fourth person turned out to be Jose.

'I could not leave,' said Jose. 'I could

not leave until I knew that the boys were safe. Now that Miguel and Pablo are reunited with their mothers, there is only Maria, the old man and me remaining, and no matter what Maria says she must also leave. I fear the old man has only a few hours to live. He is to die anyway, even if we stay with him. To move him would certainly kill him but we must go. It would be as well if we simply left him to what is inevitable. Maria, she says we cannot do this, she believes we do not have the right to do such a thing. In a way I agree with her, we should allow the Good Lord to decide.'

'It's your decision, not the decision of any god you might believe in,' said Brogan. 'Personally I don't see as it matters that much. What does matter is where are the others, how far away are they? They must come back.'

'Three, perhaps four hours' walking,' said Jose. 'At present they rest alongside a river, but I do not know for how long. Several of the children are very sick. It is too hot for them to travel, they need rest. I think they will stay there for a few days more.'

'Not too far away,' said Brogan. 'Can you persuade them to come back? I think it's important.'

'There is nothing they want more,' admitted Jose, 'but you have heard what Señor Brindley had to say. He threatened to kill every man, woman and child and I believe that he will do this.'

'That's what he's threatened to do,' admitted Brogan, 'but believe me, there is no way he can afford to do it.'

'I wish I had your faith,' said Jose.

'It ain't a matter of faith,' said Brogan. 'Take me to the others. I'll see if I can talk them into coming back. I'll explain things on the way.'

'Señor Brogan,' said Maria. 'If we are all to return to Los Cahuillas, there seems little point in my going. I will wait here with Señor Callista.'

'That is something only you can decide,' said Jose. 'I might be your guardian but you have long had a mind of your own. Perhaps Señor McNally is right and you will be safe. However, even if they do not kill you, I fear for your virtue.'

'A woman can live without her virtue,' replied Maria. 'I sometimes think it is something only men consider important. Now do not waste time, go and bring the others back. Señor Brogan, he must have good reason for wanting this. I do not believe that he would deliberately put anyone in danger.'

'Sí, you are probably right, I also do not believe he would.' Jose sighed. 'About your virtue, I suppose it is possible you are right about that too. You are usually right about most things.'

'OK,' said Brogan. 'Now we've got that sorted out, let's go. The quicker we get there the quicker we can get back.'

'As you know, I have ridden a horse before but I am not very good,' said Jose. 'I am more used to the size and pace of a mule or a donkey. But provided we do not travel too fast I will be all right.'

Just beyond the village they came across the boys and their mothers. Jose told them to return to the village and, after a somewhat confused conversation, they reluctantly agreed. Brogan gave both boys very strict orders not to leave the village and to do exactly what they were told to do. They both willingly agreed but Brogan could not help but wonder whether they would.

Travelling by horse, even fairly slowly, had the advantage of converting a three- or four-hour walk into a ride of just over an an hour. When they reached them, all the villagers immediately gathered round Brogan and Jose.

When Brogan had explained the situation to them and had given enough time for the prospect of what was planned to sink in, he reminded them of the probable riches to be gained and asked them to vote on returning to Los Cahuillas. He was not too surprised when the decision was unanimously in favour.

Even though some of the children

were very obviously ill, there was no time wasted in everyone gathering their children and belongings together and starting the trek back.

'How far away are the others?' asked Brogan.

'Not too far,' said Jose. 'Perhaps as far again.'

'Then you ride out there an' make 'em come back,' said Brogan. 'If everybody's there it'll make Brindley's claim that much more difficult to prove. I still don't believe he will try to kill anyone.'

Jose rode on and Brogan returned to Los Cahuillas where he was not at all surprised to discover that Miguel and Pablo had already disappeared. In a way, he was quite pleased; he knew that they would let him know the moment anyone else came within sight.

Eventually the boys did return and excitedly announced that a coach was approaching. Brogan had fully expected James Brindley to be the first to show himself but the arrival of the coach was unexpected, especially as it arrived from the north, the opposite direction from which he had expected anyone to come.

Not knowing who they were or even whether they had any connection with James Brindley, he decided that for the moment it might be better if he did not show himself. He hid in the church. He also told Maria, Miguel and Pablo and the two women to remain inside their adobes.

Three men clambered out of the coach, stretched themselves, dusted themselves down, and one relieved himself against the church wall. The coach driver led his charges across to the water-trough.

'I told you we'd be too early,' said one of them. 'Brindley said to be here tomorrow at the earliest.'

'Mr Wallace,' said one of the others. 'I realize that you think this is all a waste of time, but may I remind you that it isn't James Brindley who is paying out all that money. I decided to come early simply because I had very serious doubts about all this. Both Donald and myself have the feeling that all is not as it might seem. I for one didn't trust Brindley from the first time I saw him. However, it looks as though my doubts might have been misplaced, the place is obviously deserted. There isn't even the odd chicken. Mind you, the very absence of any life at all makes me wonder. Where has everybody gone?'

'I agree with you, Charles,' said the third man. 'It simply doesn't seem right that a village such as this should suddenly be empty. The last time we came it was quite a thriving community. Like most similar places it was poor, but thriving. There's something completely unnatural about it all.'

'It strikes me,' said the man who had spoken first, who was, apparently, named Mr Wallace, 'that you two are getting soft in your old age. You don't mean to tell me that you give a damn about the Mexicans or Indians or whatever they are or where or why they've gone?'

'I do not believe that either myself or Donald have any particular concern as to what has happened to the villagers,' said Charles, 'but we cannot afford to become involved in anything which might be construed to be in any way illegal.'

'I suppose not,' agreed Mr Wallace. 'But might I point out that we are not lawyers and therefore not qualified to make a decision.'

'You make it sound so very simple, Mr Wallace,' said Donald. 'Would that it were actually so. May I also remind you that Charles does have some considerable experience of the law. He is a part-time judge.'

'Very well, perhaps Charles does have some knowledge and experience,' said Mr Wallace, 'but in my opinion you are both looking for difficulties where there is none. The plight of the villagers is not our concern.'

By that time Brogan had heard enough and decided that it was time to show himself.

'Sorry there was nobody here to meet you,' he said, stepping from the church. 'Most of 'em will be back in about another two or three hours. There's more but they won't be back for about another day.'

'And who, may I ask, are you?' demanded Charles. 'You are certainly not a Mexican.'

'McNally's the name,' replied Brogan, touching the brim of his hat. 'Brogan McNally. No, sir, I ain't no Mexican. I don't have nothin' to do with Los Cahuillas either, 'ceptin' I been helpin' them against James Brindley.'

'Helping them *against* Brindley?' queried Charles. 'Do they need any help?' He looked Brogan up and down rather scathingly. 'You are plainly nothing more than what they call a saddle tramp. Even if they do need some help, do you seriously believe they'd look to the likes of you to help them?'

'I knows so,' said Brogan 'Strangely enough, they seem to trust me. The fact is they're bein' forced to leave their land by Brindley. I've been listenin' to what you was sayin an' you is right not to trust Brindley. As far as I know, at this moment he don't even own this land. I think he's meetin' with some-body from the authorities to get that little oversight put right but I ain't sure when or where that meetin' will take place. I even thought maybe it was you, but I can see that ain't so. Thing is, I understand that the village had to be deserted before he could file his claim so I reckon he should be meetin' somebody right here.'

'Well, it certainly looks deserted,' said Charles.

'He ordered everybody out of the village on pain of slaughterin' 'em all,' said Brogan.

'I find that hard to believe,' said Mr Wallace. 'People just don't go around killing other people like that these days.'

'Don't you believe it,' said Brogan. 'I've been around too long an' seen too much to believe that. It's a strange fact, but some of the worst are men just like you in fancy suits. You're right, times've changed. It used to be outlaws or bandits, but not any more. Right now though, the only law in these parts is the law of the gun. Do any of you speak Spanish?'

'Only a few words,' admitted Charles. 'You interest me, Mr McNally, or should I say what you have to say interests me.'

'There's a young girl and a couple of older women still in the village,' said Brogan. 'The older women speak no English but the young girl is near 'nough word perfect. You need to talk to her, you might be interested in what she has to say. I assume that you gentlemen are from the railroad companies?'

'You know about that?' said Charles, looking rather alarmed. 'How did you know? We told Brindley not to tell a soul.' He suddenly seemed uncomfortable and hastily added: 'For purely business reasons, you understand. We do not have any personal interest in the fate of the village or its occupants.'

'Maybe not,' said Brogan, plainly sceptical. 'To be fair though, he didn't say a thing. All the villagers had was a map with two lines drawn on it an' a date to be out of the village. A date imposed by Brindley. I just happened to be here, my horse lost a shoe an' I was lookin' for somebody to fix it. They told me what was happenin an' I got to wonderin' just why Brindley wanted this land so bad. The map and the lines on it looked just like railroads to me. Don't ask me where they got the map from.'

Suddenly the two boys, Miguel and Pablo appeared.

'Señor Brindley,' gasped Miguel, 'he come with many men. He come very fast. I think he look for you, Señor Brogan.'

'I thought I told you two to stay with your mothers?' scolded Brogan.

'My mother she say I am a big nuisance,' replied Miguel, giving a laugh. 'She tell me and Pablo to go and play somewhere. We decide to go back along the pass. We not get very far when we see Señor Brindley coming so we run very fast to tell you. He will be here very soon.'

'Gentlemen,' said Brogan. 'I do believe that your worries about Mr Brindley are about to be confirmed. Until very recently me and these two boys were being held prisoner at his ranch. As you can see, we escaped. I don't expect you take my word for that, of course, an' I don't care.'

'*Sí*, it is true, Señor Brogan, he speak true,' added Miguel. 'We are locked away. Then I have the idea to drop the bucket.'

'Drop the bucket?' queried the man named Donald. 'What the hell is the boy talking about?'

'It'll take too long to explain,' said Brogan. 'Maybe later. We should have company pretty soon now.'

'So Mr Brindley is coming. He will, of course, admit to all you claim?' said Mr Wallace, with a sneer.

'I doubt it,' said Brogan. 'But, since he's on his way here and probably doesn't know you are here, it might be a good opportunity to discover the truth of what happened for yourselves.'

'And how will we do that?' demanded Mr Wallace.

'Might I suggest that you hide up somewhere an' listen to what he has to say. Inside the church is as good a place as any.'

'He'll know we're here,' replied Charles. 'The coach.'

'Miguel,' said Brogan, 'You two are very resourceful, is there anywhere the coach can be got out of sight?'

'*Sí, señor*,' said Miguel. 'There is a barn behind those adobes.' He pointed behind him. 'It is small and there is not much room but I think it will fit inside and not be seen.'

'Then order your driver to go where the boy says,' Brogan said to Charles. 'Tell him to keep his horses quiet.'

'This is all a a complete waste of time if you ask me. It can all be resolved quite easily if you ask Mr Brindley,' muttered Mr Wallace.

'Nobody's asking you, Mr Wallace,' snapped Charles. 'I am beginning to wonder which side you are on. If we had listened to you we would have paid James Brindley with no further questions long ago. Kindly remember that it is our shareholders' money that stands to be lost.'

'I resent the implication of what you are saying,' said Mr Wallace. 'Very well, do things your way. I shall expect your apology when James Brindley is proved innocent.'

'And I shall be the first to offer that apology,' Charles assured him.

Charles ordered the coach driver to do as the boys said and in a few minutes there was no sign of it. Brogan's keen ears then picked up the sound of approaching horses and told the newcomers to hide in the church but to remain completely silent and listen. About two or three minutes later James Brindley and his men galloped through the ford.

Brindley seemed very surprised when Brogan simply stood his ground and, although all his men had drawn their guns, he motioned them not to shoot. Brogan was very quickly surrounded.

'McNally,' said Brindley. 'I must admit that either you have one hell of a nerve or you are very foolish. I do not believe you are a fool. You must've heard us coming. Why didn't you run for it?'

'Run?' asked Brogan. 'Mr Brindley, one thing I've never done in my life is run. Besides, where would I run to?' He waved his arm around. 'If you and your men know this territory as well as you claim, you would soon find me.'

'Very true,' admitted Brindley. 'You know, I always had the feeling that you would somehow manage to escape but I just didn't see how. You are a very resourceful man. What does surprise me is the fact that you have not made good your escape, that you have allowed yourself to be caught again. Perhaps you are not as clever as you thought you were.'

'Maybe that ought to tell you somethin',' said Brogan.

'Tell me what?' demanded Brindley.

'Never mind,' said Brogan. 'If you are expecting the villagers to give up so easy, then you've got things all wrong. Most of 'em should be back here any time now and the others by tomorrow mornin' at the latest. Maybe even tonight.'

'And why should that bother me?'

'Because you wanted a deserted village.'

'Their return is a mere trifling inconvenience,' said Brindley. 'Unfortunately for them — and for you — I shall have no alternative but to kill them all. I didn't want to do it, but under the circumstances I must.'

'That's an awful lot of bodies to get rid of,' said Brogan. 'Slaughter on that scale leaves a lot of tell-tale signs and somehow such things can never be kept secret. What will you do with the bodies and how will you explain them?'

'You plainly don't know the area,' said Brindley. 'There is a ravine about two miles away. The bodies will be thrown down there. After that it won't take the foxes and vultures long to dispose of them and those who aren't eaten will soon rot in this heat. After a few days there won't even be any bones left. Besides, there is nobody to find them. Nobody will even notice they are missing.

'The vultures will soon be seen,' said Brogan.

'Whatever happens, it won't bother you,' said Brindley. 'Your body will be one of them.'

'Maybe,' said Brogan. 'Anyhow, I know about the railroads.' Brindley looked alarmed for a moment. 'I know about them crossin' right here an' that whoever owns this land stands to make a lot of money.'

'You think you know,' said Brindley. 'I said you weren't a fool but I have changed my mind, you *are* a fool,

McNally. You might be very resourceful and even clever, but still a fool. Had things been done my way the villagers would have remained alive but now that you have interfered they must die. Because you are such a resourceful man, Mr McNally, I shall not allow you the luxury of puttng off your death any longer. I have seen just how stupid that would be. I intend to make certain that you die right here and now while I watch you die. As you can see, there are nine guns aimed at you. They can't all miss from this range.'

'The first man who shoots will face a charge of murder!' a voice suddenly thundered from the church. Charles and Donald appeared in the doorway. 'As well as being an official of the railroad company, Mr Brindley, I am also a part-time judge. You men, put away your guns and nothing more will happen to you.'

Most of the men glanced at James Brindley and were plainly alarmed. After few moments of uncertainty, all but two holstered their guns and these two — one of them being Jake — looked questioningly at Brindley. However, those few seconds' delay meant that they were too late. Brogan had drawn his gun and it was aimed steadily at Brindley.

'You'll be the first to die, Brindley,' said Brogan. 'I never miss from as close as this.'

Suddenly Brindley laughed loudly and shook his head. He actually appeared genuinely amused. 'Hell, McNally, you must have been spawned by the devil himself. Somebody or somethin' is sure looking after you. I just wish I had one tenth of your luck, I'd be the richest man in the world. Don't shoot,' he ordered his men. 'He means what he says.' He raised his hat slightly and spoke to the railroad men. 'Good afternoon, Mr Godley, Mr Forgan,' he said to Charles and Donald. 'I wasn't expecting you, you're a day early. I know how things must look but surely you don't believe a word this no-good saddle tramp has told you?'

'On its own, perhaps not,' admitted Charles. 'But we did hear what you just said about killing the Mexicans. I think we have heard enough.'

'I think we ought to listen to Mr Brindley's explanation first,' said Mr Wallace, emerging from the church, gun in hand. 'I'm sure Mr Brindley didn't really mean he was going to kill them. It was probably a figure of speech. I for one would rather take the word of somebody like Mr Brindley than a dirty, smelly saddle tramp or even a Mexican peon.'

'You would,' said Donald. 'Actually I have had my suspicions about you for some time. I think it's you who have some explaining to do. How much was Brindley paying you?'

'Enough,' admitted Mr Wallace. 'Now, Mr McNally, it would appear that we have something of a stalemate. Your gun is aimed at Mr Brindley and my gun is aimed at Charles Godley, the question is, who dies first?'

'Either way I would suggest it was the deal you had with Brindley that was dead,' said Brogan.

'Not so,' replied Wallace. 'In fact I had allowed for just such a situation. I didn't expect it to happen, one never does, but I always imagine the worst possible scenario. It is all very simple really. We met with Mr Brindley, the deal was signed but suddenly and for no apparent reason, we were attacked. True, I had not imagined somebody like you, but a saddle tramp will do just fine. Unfortunately Mr Godley and Mr Forgan were killed. However, the deal had been signed and is therefore still quite legal.'

'Except that we haven't signed yet,' reminded Charles. 'Under the circumstances it is most unlikely we shall sign. I must remind you that all three signatures are required.'

'A minor detail,' said Wallace with a dry laugh. 'Amongst my lesser-known skills is being a very good forger. I have been practising your signatures and I have even tried them out, unbeknown to you. Nothing that would attract any undue attention but enough to test my skill. There is no way anyone will be able to tell the difference.'

Although Brogan was watching Brindley, the actions of others did not go unobserved. Jake and the other man with his gun were some distance away from Brindley but, in the corner of his eye, Brogan saw Jake raise his gun, albeit slightly. He saw that the gun was aimed at him.

★ ★ ★

Brogan later had to admit that Jake was good and fast but luckily for him he, Brogan, was faster and even more accurate.

He felt Jake's bullet slam into his upper left arm, although there was no real pain, simply a strangely warm sensation as blood seeped into his sleeve. The bullet from Brogan's long-barrelled Navy Colt, on the other hand, drilled a neat hole in Jake's forehead.

There was only the merest hint of blood as Jake slowly toppled, wide-eyed but sightless from his horse. A fraction of a second after his first shot and before Jake had fallen from his horse, the second man also died as Brogan fired again. This time the bullet thudded into the man's chest.

Things had happened so quickly that Wallace did not react. When he did move he found himself staring into the barrel of Brogan's gun.

'Two down,' said Brogan. 'Do you want to be number three?'

'What the hell are you all waiting for?' Brindley shouted at his men. 'Kill the bastard!'

'No sir, Mr Brindley,' replied one of them. 'We ain't about to try to kill nobody. You don't pay us enough to die. You is on your own, we've all had enough. You want him dead, you kill him.'

'Yes, sir,' said another. 'We'd all already decided that we warn't goin' to kill no Mexicans either. We ain't no angels, none of us, but killin' on that scale . . . Hell, we just ain't into that kind of slaughter. Anyhow there warn't no way you could've gotten away with it even in this god-forsaken territory. McNally was right, things like that always seem to get about.'

'No, sir,' said the first man. 'Like I say, you is on your own now, all of you, you too, McNally. We're gettin' the hell out of here while we can. Come on, boys,' he said to the others. 'First stop, the ranch, to collect our things an' see what there is worth takin' in lieu of the money he owes us.'

'I'll see you all dead!' shouted Brindley. 'Don't any of you dare touch one thing on my ranch. It's all mine.'

Several of the men laughed. 'Reckon you can stop us?' called one. 'We just might make an exception to no killin' in your case.'

By that time, Donald Forgan had taken the gun off a now very bemused Mr Wallace, but James Brindley screamed some obscenity at the men and clumsily drew his gun.

It was Brogan who reacted first. His single shot sent Brindley's pistol flying through the air and blood spurting from Brindley's hand.

'I could've killed you easy enough,' Brogan pointed out. 'I just thought it might be better if you was made to face trial, though. Mr Godley bein' a judge an' all that, I reckon he knows how to handle these things. I ain't no lawyer but I reckon that's what he had in mind.'

'Nice shootin', McNally,' said one of the men. 'You saved us a job. OK, boys, let's get the hell out of here an' see what we can find at the ranch.'

'I can't stop you,' said Charles Godley. 'I don't intend to try either. All I will ask is that you do not destroy anything, particularly any papers. They could prove vital in court.'

'You got our word on that,' promised the first man. 'Can't say as there might not be a few things busted though.

Some of us is a mite clumsy at times an' Brindley does have some good whiskey locked away. Anyhow, I don't think any of us can read or write all that good, I know I can't. The only kind of papers we're interested in is any with dollar or maybe peso signs an' numbers on it. Don't you worry none, we're all expert at readin' when it comes to paper money.'

'I know I can't force you, but I might need you to testify against Brindley,' said Charles Godley. 'Somebody will have to swear to the court that he intended to kill the villagers. At the very least somebody will have to testify that he tried to drive them out of the village.'

'Then it looks like you got yourself a problem,' sneered the man. 'Ain't one of us would be willin' to speak in no court. Most of us is only used to bein' up for trial. We wouldn't trust no judge. Come on boys, let's go.'

Most of the men whooped with delight at the prospect of ransacking

Brindley's ranch as they turned their horses and spurred them forward. In a matter of minutes they were out of sight.

'Well, Mr Brindley,' said Charles Godley when things had quietened down. 'It looks like the end of the line for you and Mr Wallace. Mr McNally tells me he thinks you had arranged to meet somebody here to finalize the selling of this land.'

'A pox on you, McNally,' rasped Brindley. 'I would say I hope you rot in hell but I reckon you'd be at home there.'

'I guess I'm just lucky sometimes,' said Brogan. He suddenly listened. 'Sounds like we got company comin' in. It ain't any of Brindley's men, they went in the opposite direction.'

In answer to his observation two riders appeared. Brogan noticed that one appeared to be wearing the badge of a lawman. Both were plainly very concerned at what greeted them and the other man looked hard and quizzically at Brindley.

'You have very acute hearing, Mr McNally,' remarked Charles Godley. 'I don't think anyone else heard them.'

'Yes, sir,' said Brogan rather boastfully, 'I can hear a fly land on a piece of shit a hundred yards away.' He nodded at the two new arrivals. 'Looks like you had yourselves a wasted journey. Los Cahuillas ain't deserted. There's still a few here an' the others will all be back by tomorrow mornin' at the latest. Most are already on their way here.'

'Brindley?' asked one of the men, looking questioningly at James Brindley. It was Charles Godley who answered.

'I see that you, sir,' he said to the second man, 'wear the badge of a lawman. May I ask your name?'

'Deputy Marshal Willis Craythorne,' replied the man. 'Would somebody please explain what the hell's goin' on here?' James Brindley, Charles Godley and Mr Wallace started talking at the same time. 'Now just hold on!' ordered the marshal. 'One at a time. You, sir.' He indicated Charles Godley. 'What's your name? Let's hear what you have to say.'

Charles Godley told the marshal who he was, why he was in Los Cahuillas and what had happened since his arrival. He stressed the fact that he was also a part-time judge, something which did not seem to impress the marshal. Both James Brindley and Mr Wallace tried to interrupt but were silenced by the marshal. Eventually James Brindley was allowed to speak.

James Brindley actually said very little in defence of himself, most of his tirade was directed at Brogan. Mr Wallace, of course, denied any connection with Brindley. Eventually the marshal spoke to Brogan.

'It strikes me that you are just about the only one here who does not seem to have any vested interest,' he said. 'Let me hear your version of what happened.'

'A saddlebum!' exploded Brindley.

'That's all he is, a filthy saddle tramp. You can't rely on the word of somebody like him.'

'Maybe he is a saddlebum,' observed the marshal. 'Does that make him a liar? As I see it he is just about the only one of you who don't have a reason. Let's hear what he has to say.'

★   ★   ★

James Brindley and Mr Wallace — his first name was actually Arthur — had been arrested by the marshal and negotiations between the villagers and the railroad companies had opened almost immediately.

Brogan and a few of the villagers had, somewhat reluctantly, agreed to give evidence at the trial of the two men which, thankfully for him, took place only a week later. More surprisingly, both Helen and Nathaniel also gave evidence against their former employer. Both men were found guilty of various offences — most of which even Brogan failed to understand.

Brogan had at first been puzzled as to why Deputy Marshal Willis Craythorne had been involved. It turned out that it was simply because the marshal had been reluctant to believe that the villagers would willingly leave their village. He had decided to make certain.

After the trial, at which Jose represented the village, Brogan had ridden back. He had no particular reason for returning to Los Cahuillas, Brogan McNally was most definitely not a person who enjoyed farewells. In truth it was probably simply because that was the direction in which he had originally been travelling.

Whilst his arrival was greeted with a certain amount of enthusiasm, the majority of the villagers were plainly far more concerned with the prospect of great riches than with showing any real gratitude towards Brogan. Brogan ruefully observed that memories were very short. In fact the only three who seemed genuinely pleased to see him were Maria and the two boys, Miguel and Pablo. Maria was a little sad that the old man, Seve Callista, had died whilst Brogan had been away. The two boys wanted to pack their bags and follow him. He made his remark about short memories to Maria.

'Sí,' she sighed, 'it is very true, people, they have very short memories. At first I thought it would be a good thing when the railroads come to Los Cahuillas, now I am not so sure. Already many people have changed. As yet they do not have the money but already they are spending it in their minds. Now, brother fights with brother about who actually owns what. I am afraid, Señor Brogan, that while Señor Brindley might not have succeeded in driving us out or slaughtering us, Los Cahuillas has ceased to exist in anything but name. The mighty dollar has succeeded in killing the spirit of every man, woman and child in Los Cahuillas where even Señor Brindley failed. It is not man, it is money that has murdered Los Cahuillas. Perhaps it would have been better for us to leave. We might have remained real people.'

'I know exactly how you feel,' said Brogan. 'Maybe that's why I'm a saddlebum. Life is simpler that way.'

THE END

We do hope that you have enjoyed reading this large print book.

Did you know that all of our titles are available for purchase?

We publish a wide range of high quality large print books including:
Romances, Mysteries, Classics
General Fiction
Non Fiction and Westerns

Special interest titles available in large print are:
The Little Oxford Dictionary
Music Book, Song Book
Hymn Book, Service Book

Also available from us courtesy of Oxford University Press:
Young Readers' Dictionary
(large print edition)
Young Readers' Thesaurus
(large print edition)

For further information or a free brochure, please contact us at:
Ulverscroft Large Print Books Ltd.,
The Green, Bradgate Road, Anstey,
Leicester, LE7 7FU, England.
Tel: (00 44) **0116 236 4325**
Fax: (00 44) **0116 234 0205**

VENGEANCE AT BITTERSWEET

Dale Graham

Always a loner, Largo reckoned it was the reason for his survival as a bounty hunter. But things change when he has to join forces with Colonel Sebastian Kyte in the hunt for a band of desperate killers. Kyte is not interested in financial rewards. So what is the old Confederate soldier's game? And how does a Kiowa medicine man's daughter figure in the final showdown at Bittersweet? Vengeance is sweet, but it comes with a heavy price tag.

DEVIL'S RANGE

Skeeter Dodds

Caleb Ross had agreed to join his old friend Tom Watson as a ranching partner in Ghost Creek, and arrives full of optimism. But he rides into big trouble. Tom has been gunned down by Jack Sweeney of the Rawl range, mentor in mayhem to Scott Rawl . . . Enraged, Caleb heads for the ranch seeking vengeance for Tom's murder. But, up against a crooked law force and formidable opposition, he'll have to be quick and clever if he's to survive . . .